Sometimes, you need to leave the bad things in the past.

Art smiled, but it didn't get anywhere within a mile of his eyes.

"I have to ask if this is something you're willing to take on, Mark. I'm not fibbing or lying or anything else when I say I'd understand if you're not. Whatever's up there half scared the life out of me. You ever feel that way about a place?"

This time Mark did shiver, and he didn't try to hide it. Maybe it was time he admitted at least a bit of what he and Beth (and Clina) had actually gotten into back in December.

"Just one time. When we were taking your lost miner's bones out of that old house pit. I was sure then and I'm more sure now that he dropped the rock that hit Beth on purpose. Thing is, I know in my bones that the rock was really aimed at me."

Secrets in the Land: Book Two of the Voices through Time Series

Copyright © 2019 by Kari A. Kilgore

All rights reserved

Published 2019 by Spiral Publishing, Ltd.
www.spiralpublishing.net
St. Paul, Virginia

Book and cover design copyright © 2019 by Spiral Publishing, Ltd.

Cover art copyright © 2019 by serg-nester | Depositphotos.com

ISBN-13: 978-1-948890-22-9
Large Print ISBN-13: 978-1-948890-29-8

LOC NUMBER: 2019912082

This book is licensed for your personal enjoyment only. All rights reserved. This is a work of fiction. All characters and events portrayed in this book are fictional, and any resemblance to real people or incidents is purely coincidental. This book, or parts thereof, may not be reproduced in any form without permission.

To Dallas

*For all the love, support, and friendship over the years,
despite a rather unfortunate incident the first time we met.*

SECRETS IN THE LAND

BOOK TWO OF THE VOICES THROUGH TIME
SERIES

KARI KILGORE

SPIRAL PUBLISHING, LTD.

Chapter 1

EVEN AFTER A DECADE of living away and more frequent visits over the last few months, something in Mark Hersch's shoulders unknotted every time he crossed back over into Boun County, Virginia.

Making the trip for work and not only for a much anticipated visit with Beth Azen, his girlfriend of the past few months, made no difference. Much as he looked forward to a surprise visit with her after too many weeks apart for his taste, this was something more.

Maybe it was the view from the high gap as the road wound through the rugged mountains of his home county. This time of year, the trees up on the distant ridgeline still showed faint pink buds, while the oaks, maples, and poplars that crowded the four lane flashed the vivid pale green of new leaves.

The mountains themselves always looked like rolling ocean waves from up here no matter how much he'd learned over the years about plate tectonics and erosion and exactly how the wild landscape had taken shape.

The deep blue late winter sky looked huge from up here,

too, enough that he could see a low line of dark clouds in the distance. Plenty of time left for an early March snow. And the welcome possibility of cuddling with Beth and her sweet hound dog Janie by the wood stove.

Maybe his bone-deep relaxation was due to the quiet, with the constant traffic and noise of Richmond hours behind him. Or the earthy, rich smell of the forest around him coming to life after the long, especially snowy winter. He knew exactly *how* snowy since he'd slogged through it for quick weekend visits more times than he could count.

The lingering chill against his face when he rolled the window down was well worth it for that first welcome-home breath. The contrast with the vehicle exhaust and overly conditioned indoor air around his city digs had his sinuses singing hallelujah, especially since the pollen frenzy hadn't really kicked in at the higher elevations yet.

Mark inhaled the fresh mountain air again before he closed the window, shifting into a more comfortable road-trip slouch in the blue Commonwealth of Virginia sedan. He brushed his hand through his more unruly than usual reddish-blond hair and laughed out loud at his strong impulse to shed the strangling tie he'd never quite gotten used to and unbutton his dress shirt.

He did both and immediately felt a whole lot better.

Yeah, it was beautiful here. And while he could finally see the end of the long-distance part of a relationship with a woman he never wanted to be away from for more than a few hours, Mark was twitchy as a schoolboy at the thought of seeing Beth.

But he knew the reaction of his mind, his body, and even his heart had a good bit to do with getting back home.

He glanced at the white cardboard box full of files in the passenger seat and grinned. After thinking and planning and writing and talking about it for years, all at once Mark's dream project felt close enough to touch.

Each carefully labeled folder in the box stamped with the blue logo for the Department of Mines, Minerals, and Energy was full of his neat handwriting, printed sheets covered with spreadsheet data, and topographical maps he knew as well as the back roads through Boun County. He could call the locations and specifications for all the mining sites old or new throughout the coalfields to mind without a whole lot of effort.

He'd spent the last decade coordinating between the coalfields and the capitol on reclaiming or sometimes re-mining the old sites. The big ones, anyway. The projects that made a real difference and gave a great return for the taxpayer dollar in cleaning up eyesores and giving back flat, usable land in a region that truly needed it.

But Mark's professional passion—and he knew perfectly well why some of his co-workers changed the word to obsession—was cleaning up waterways long spoiled by mine runoff. Especially the creeks and streams around his family's home in Hartstown.

He was still amazed at how years of suggesting at least a side focus on the small, unpermitted house pits that kept those tributaries of the bigger rivers fouled had paid off all at once. Well, not exactly all at once, and not without the intervention of meeting Beth and getting to know her unstoppable drive and determination to solve the mystery of a century of tragedy and loss in Hartstown.

More tragedy and heartbreak than any little town should have had to live through.

And of course, the shock, surprise, and delightful acceptance of the unorthodox and particularly Appalachian way Beth had led the way to that solution.

Either way, the positive publicity—for the Commonwealth, Boun County, and Mark's boss at DMME—generated by the discovery and proper burial of a long-lost miner had accelerated Mark's timeline considerably.

But he'd still been surprised when Mike Powell had sprung the trip that morning without even a hint of warning. He'd just waved Mark out with a strange twinkle in his eye, and all he would say was a local boy had to investigate this one.

Or at least an Air Force brat who'd grown up coming home to Hartstown for major holidays and summer vacation no matter where he attended school that year.

And maybe a local boy who was head over his fool heels in love enough to take every spare moment he got to make the drive. Powell had suspected Mark would jump at the chance, and he hadn't been wrong.

Mark hit the turn signal at the green sign that declared the next exit would bring him to Hartstown in seven miles, strangely reluctant to end what had been an unusually pleasant surprise road trip. But now he followed the twisting road over and through the high gap, then down into the close, deep valleys of home.

Besides, if this project went as well as the last few had, his long-held daydream of getting himself assigned to the neglected Boun County field office just might come true sooner than he'd dared hope it would. Before the end of autumn looked likely. Sooner seemed possible.

When he finally drove through the long, sweeping curve from the four-lane to two-lane road that would shortly turn into Hartstown's Main Street, Mark glanced at his phone long enough to tap the Favorites list. Beth's lovely smiling face popped up at the very top.

Her low, sexy voice filled the car's speakers after only one ring.

"Hey there handsome!"

"Hey yourself, gorgeous. How's the arm holding up?"

She half sighed, half growled. Mark wondered if she had any idea what that did to parts of him best ignored while he was driving.

He knew better than to ask.

"Making me crazy, to tell you the truth. The physical therapy plan seems to be to tear my shoulder all to pieces when all I want to do is get my hand strong again. All those weeks hanging in a sling makes me feel like I have two dumb hands instead of one. I guess I should be thankful the damn brace is finally off."

"I'm sorry, sweetheart. You just started this week, right?"

Mark grinned when she blew air out through her lips loud enough that he heard it. And once again, the thought of her full, curving lips perked up the horny teenaged boy crouched inside him.

He slowed to twenty-five miles an hour as he got into town, eyes on the squat red brick town hall a few blocks away. The 1980s construction stood out from the surprising number of Hartstown's beautiful historic buildings that were made of pale gray stone built by immigrants from all over the world. Intricate carvings and decorations as fine as anything in Richmond or anywhere else reflected the pride of those workers a hundred years in their graves.

He and Beth had learned more than anyone would have ever imagined about Boun County's original settlers—and their graves—back in December.

When she'd broken her arm saving his life inside what had to be one of the whole Southeast's most mysterious (and honestly, truly haunted) old house coal pits.

The same week she'd captured his heart.

"Yeah, yeah," she said, "be patient and let my shoulder get stronger, let everything finish healing, and all that. I know. Where does our fair Commonwealth have you off to today?"

"Oh, you know. The usual. Down 81, up 77. Little jaunt along 19."

Beth let out her full and joyful laugh, something he knew from about a thousand phone conversations that she hardly ever did in the quiet town hall.

"Andrew Mark Hersch, you are a devious and purely evil man. You're *here*?"

"Rolling down Main Street. I would have strolled right in and surprised you, but you forbade me to ever do that again after Valentine's Day. Upon pain of death, if I remember correctly."

She made a rude raspberry noise into the phone, particularly effective through the car's bass speakers, and he heard her call out to someone that she'd be back in a bit.

"Well, I can hardly welcome you back home in the manner you deserve in the middle of the office, can I? Where are you?"

Just as he'd hoped, she pushed open the brown steel front door (still with her hip rather than her right arm) at the same time he pulled into one of the diagonal parking spots a few feet away.

He could tell himself it wouldn't happen this time all he wanted. Remind himself that he was thirty-six years old and not a punky kid with his first crush.

But dependable as the sun rising in the morning, Mark's heart sped up, and slow, delicious heat rose in his belly when he saw her.

Curly brown hair lifting in the breeze. Faded blue jeans and his ancient, nearly pink Virginia Tech t-shirt that draped across her tall, slender frame just right. Her arm finally out of the bulky cast and the hard brace she'd worn for too long.

And a huge grin lighting her face and her gorgeous blue eyes, brighter than any sunrise Mark had ever seen.

"I'm right here," he said before he ended the call and got out.

Two steps for each of them and Beth was finally warm and real and coffee-scented in his arms, grabbing her own wrist and squeezing him hard enough that his road-weary back crackled. He luxuriated in the sensation of both her arms around his body instead of only one for so many weeks.

Her lips brushed his neck and ear on the way to his mouth, sending delightful chills along his arms and legs.

"*Now* I'm home," he whispered against her cheek before he kissed her long and proper.

Beth drew back, breathless and laughing, her cheeks flushed.

"You certainly are. And who should I thank for this mid-week treat?"

"Our old buddy Art Steffens, for one. My boss, too. Are you on your usual crazy schedule and haven't had lunch yet? I bolted out of Richmond in way too much of a hurry to take time to stop."

She smiled and kissed the tip of his nose.

"As usual, and just in time for our usual. Rayburn's it is."

Chapter 2

MARK HAD NEVER QUITE figured out what it was about the tiny little Italian place in Hartstown that made it so damn good. Rayburn's looked like any of the hundreds of similar joints in small towns across the country. Red vinyl booths and Formica tables sat under murals full of scenes straight out of an old movie melodrama about ancient Roman gods and goddesses and their complicated love lives.

But he had to admit the more-vivid-than-life images seemed romantic and wistful rather than amateurish or overdone. Those paintings were more like what he wished he could see in Italy instead of the tourist-packed reality he'd experienced on a trip with his family while his father was stationed in Germany.

Several huge televisions hanging from the ceiling should have destroyed the ambiance of the place, but the volume was almost always muted. On days like today when no big sports game of any kind was available, the sets were tuned to travelogue videos of Rome, Florence, Pompeii, and other spots Mark couldn't identify.

And the *food*. Even with all the traveling he'd been lucky

enough to do while his Dad was in the Air Force, Mark would happily swear he'd never had a better straight-up pepperoni pizza than the ones they served at Rayburn's. As always, the second he walked through the door the warm scent of baking yeast crusts and French fries and onions had his stomach growling and ornery.

"So tell me," Beth said, grabbing Mark's hands as soon as they managed to scoot into the same booth they'd had the first night they met. "What's Art got your whole agency stirred up about?"

Mark let go long enough to drain half of his Coke before he answered. The sharp scent was as refreshing as the bubbly bitter sweetness.

"It seems one of the creeks on his land has some unusual contaminant readings since that last heavy rain. Odd things showing up downstream, too." He paused, shaking his head. "Hang on, my Granny would smack me upside the head for being so rude. How are you today, Clina?"

Beth chuckled as she squeezed his hand. Clina Jane, the ghostly presence who'd managed to get through to Beth back in December, had been the one who led the way into that old house pit. The change in the bad luck that used to hover over Hartstown had been a dramatic turn for the better.

Almost as dramatic as the change in Mark's life.

He didn't have to look to know Beth wore a sparkling copper chain around her neck, with a piece of glass about the size of his thumbnail at the end, sealed and outlined with more copper. All that remained of the glass plate negative Clina had used to make contact after decades of trying.

After months and dozens of Clina's spectral comments, he knew exactly what to expect. And a little boy part of him still jumped when she spoke.

"I reckon I'm doing just fine, young feller. Glad to see

you home where you belong. Think you'll manage to stay around for good this time?"

Mark gazed into Beth's eyes, both of them smiling. While they agreed that the recurring reunions were mighty damn fine, he knew Beth was as eager as he for a more stable arrangement.

"Working on it, Clina. No one wants me back home more than I do."

"Almost no one," Beth said with a wink.

She sat back to make room for a steaming hot pepperoni pizza, breaking his contact with Clina. The waiter expertly balanced the huge round tray on a tiny metal stand in the middle of the table, dropped a stack of napkins and plates, and disappeared.

Mark resisted another little boy urge he'd fought his whole life—the desire to take a huge bite of the pizza that was currently intoxicating all of his senses, scorched tongue and mouth be damned. But the underlying and entirely grownup urge to use his mouth and tongue on Beth as much and as soon as possible forced him to be more patient than usual.

Sure enough, she watched him with a smart-ass grin. Probably remembering how many times he'd made the wrong choice while she waited patiently, and scorch-free.

"So, the creek's on Art's land?" she said.

Mark shook his head, trying to focus on this conversation and the work reason he was here instead of his anticipation of pleasant sights, sounds, and scents currently distracting him.

"Yeah, I'll need to read over the files again to make sure, but from what Powell said and from what I could see on the topo map, a mine close by might have changed the groundwater levels. Then when that big rain hit, whatever was trapped, maybe in a cave, started washing out."

"You said the washout was odd?" Beth said. "Not the usual mercury and mine runoff stuff?"

"None of that, not like with the old mine sites. The tests are picking up strange things like arsenic and formaldehyde."

Beth frowned as she slid two pieces of pizza onto each of their plates.

"I've never heard of that out of a natural cave around here."

"Nope, me neither. I don't want to get too detailed while we're eating, but they've found traces of those kinds of contaminants that don't play well with humans around old graveyards. Some as old as the Civil War."

"Yikes." She paused with her first slice of pizza halfway to her mouth and made a gagging noise. "No wonder they want someone down here to check it out."

"Not sure why they want me, though," Mark said, picking up his own pizza. "I'm used to dealing with a bunch of toxic materials, but not so much with flooded cemeteries."

They each took a huge bite, and their eyes met before they rolled closed in pleasure. After a lifetime of enjoying pizza through burn-deadened taste buds, Mark had to admit this was worth changing a bad habit for. Chewy crust rich with yeasty goodness, perfectly melty cheese, and sharp, spicy pepperoni good enough to savor, and savor often.

Beth recovered enough to speak first, probably because she could walk across the street any day of the week for this ambrosia.

"Did your manager say why they wanted you? Of course *I* want you, so I'm happy either way."

"Glad to hear that," Mark said, grinning. "All he would say is a local boy had to check this one out. To tell you the truth, I didn't ask too many questions. I pretty much ran for the car."

"I'd bet Art was one reason they picked you. He's still talking up how we found the long-lost soul on his land."

"I'd love to see his face if he ever found out he wasn't exaggerating, at least this one time."

The two of them fell into a most undignified fit of giggling, one of the many things Mark had been missing about time spent with Beth.

"How's the book going?" he said, grabbing two more pieces for each of them.

"Better now that I can use both hands." Beth waggled her right fingers, and Mark didn't miss the trembling signs of overwork. "All I could do before was scan. Very slowly and carefully. Or rig the mouse up close to my chest. Just being able to type again feels like heaven, even if I'm slower than I was in grade school."

"You'll get it back. If I know you as well as I think I do, you're probably already overdoing your physical therapy. Is Clina hearing anything new and interesting?"

Beth rolled her eyes, then she smiled and shook her head. "Only the usual chatter from Clina. Our rescued miner is doing great, hanging out with your granddad, actually. And they're both glad you're home. Almost as glad as I am."

Mark closed his eyes, not wanting to fight back tears when he'd barely gotten there. Getting to communicate with his beloved Papaw—even through Beth and Clina—had turned into one of the greatest joys of his life.

At the memory of Beth making an amusing point of taking her necklace off every time they got physical, Mark realized he'd never made love to her without having to be careful. First of her cast and then of the hard plastic brace she hated even worse. As many times as they'd been together, tonight would be the first time he'd finally get to see and touch every inch of her.

And he intended to do just that.

"If I may make a suggestion," he said, "why don't we finish up here and head back to your place? Assuming I'm invited to stay there this time."

She tapped her chin, pretending to think it over.

"Well, I suppose I can get all my other boyfriends to make other arrangements, even though it *is* short notice."

Mark nodded once. "As long as I get first priority, I'm good."

"I'd bet you could catch Art in his office while I'm wrapping up at work. Get a head start on whatever's happening, so you can focus on me this evening."

"Don't worry about my ability to focus on you. Not unless you mean my ability to focus on much of anything tomorrow after neither of us getting nearly enough sleep tonight."

Chapter 3

ART STEFFENS, a local attorney with a habit of buying up old mining or timber land to protect with conservation easements and replant with hardwoods, had an office just across from the town hall. The three story building was another newer brick structure, but this one was painted a mellow tan that set it apart from the red brick and gray stone all around.

When he'd given Mark and Beth permission to investigate his land for sources of runoff from old, unpermitted mines, Art hadn't been expecting much. Just the improvement of the waterways he worked so hard to protect and improve. Art's influence as a family friend over the years had undoubtedly helped get Mark into reclamation and protecting water himself.

But Art's low expectations back in December didn't stop him from happily telling everyone why it was worth it to allow Mark access to their land, or from having framed photos of the long-lost miner's bones in his office.

Mark stepped inside to the merry sound of the door's jingling bell, thinking how in some ways photos of a bundle of bones were the least strange things on display. Several waist-high glass and wood cases held old magazines, collections of arrowheads, a variety of coal scrip coins, and bunches of other local oddities like antique boot brushes and union hall banners.

The yellow poplar walls were hung with antique mining equipment. Some as understandable as old metal helmets and hand lanterns with red or green glass. Some likely a bit more ominous to folks who didn't know what they were looking at, like manual drills several feet long.

The whole collection always made Mark smile, and think once again that he needed to make time to let Art take him on a tour of the whole place. Since they'd crossed paths again in December and several times since, Mark had finally started thinking of Art as one of his friends more than someone his parents and grandparents knew.

The receptionist's Art Deco wooden desk was empty except for a sleek, black phone. Like many offices in Hartstown, the casual nature was a pleasant change from government formality in Richmond. Before Mark could decide whether to call and leave a message for an appointment or knock on the six-panel oak door, Art himself popped his head out.

"Mark! My favorite reclamation man!"

Art was a few inches taller than Mark, with a fuzz of steel gray hair, round rimless glasses, and a white goatee trimmed precisely enough to put Mark's neat reddish beard to shaggy shame. Rather than any kind of suit or city law firm attire, Art wore blue jeans and a green golf shirt.

He walked out and shook Mark's hand with a solid grip and waved him over to one of the burgundy couches in front of the display cases.

"Everyone took off early today, just me rattling around here by myself," Art said, beaming as if Mark were his long-lost son. "How the hell did you get here so fast?"

"I headed out first thing this morning, hit good traffic most of the way down. Figured if you were involved, I'd have something well worth the drive home."

Art laughed and shook his head. "Well, I sure do appreciate the quick response, but I know good and damn well why you really got here so fast. Not a thing in the world I could come up with that would catch your attention the way Miss Beth Azen has."

Mark held up both hands, knowing his red face gave everything away.

"You got me there, Art. I'd go a lot further a lot faster for her, and that's the truth."

Art clapped Mark on the shoulder. "Good. She's worth that and a heck of a lot more. Listen, I don't know what's going on with this creek of mine, but I don't like it. I had it tested after I bought the land like I always do, and the water smells nasty, too. I don't know of any old mines up there, but I wouldn't be surprised if there are caves nearby."

This kind of rapid change of subject was nothing new from Art, and Mark shifted right along with him.

"I had a look at those test results this morning. On the high end for sulfur, but not dangerous levels. Not that unusual for being near so many coal deposits. The arsenic and formaldehyde caught my attention a lot more."

Art nodded and scowled at the same time, puffed up his cheeks, and blew his breath out.

"I know, I know. Mike Powell probably thinks I'm trying to weasel my way into getting it set up as a Superfund site or some other such bullshit. Even if we put the test results aside, something a lot bigger is going on up there."

"Nothing else changed close by? Anything else strange going on?"

Art shook his head, frowning.

"Besides a nasty clear cut job by one of the worst crews

I've seen around here in thirty years or more? Bad enough that I'll have that agency down here to follow up soon as I'm able, and maybe bring the seller in on the results? Nothing besides more rain than we've had in years on top of one of the snowiest winters since I was a kid."

"Who found a crew that would do the job that badly?"

"I bought the land from a woman by the name of Ruddin. Melanie Ruddin, lives out in Denver. She inherited the land and a very old, very large house here in town. Burned down last autumn, I believe. I never did meet her, so I'm not sure if it was her or someone local who hired that bunch of numbskulls who made such a mess."

Mark rubbed at his eyes, hoping he wasn't about to get into a mess of his own trying to figure out who made which bad decision, and when. Hopefully that would all fall to a different state agency.

"What's your guess on the water, Art?"

"I've always thought that land sat too close to the big mines to trust the water table. That's one way I got it so cheap, because no one would build on it knowing they'd lose their groundwater. Probably sunk when Mossy Rock opened those new shafts over the winter to expand Number Four. But that wouldn't cause this new stuff to run out higher up. Damnedest thing, too, once I hiked up there to trace the creek back. Hang on just a minute."

He stood and walked back through the inner office door, and returned before Mark even wondered how long he'd be.

"Found these toward the bottom of the valley there, near where the creek comes out of the mountainside. I wore gloves and all, don't worry. Still washed my hands and everything else with the way that water stinks."

He dropped a handful of what looked like lost pearls from an old jewelry box into Mark's hand. Vaguely square and about the size of Mark's fingertip, and lumpy and ranging from white to yellow to almost brown. None of them had holes for string.

The texture seemed strange, too. Not as smooth as pears, and without the luster.

Mark shifted them in his hand and noticed several had pits and indentations, and a few of the bigger ones had black or silver around the edges. And several of them had bumps on one side.

Either two or four bumps.

A lot like something had broken off.

His full stomach turned a slow, knotty summersault.

"These look like… Art, are you thinking these are *teeth*?"

Chapter 4

ART NODDED, a grim smile on his face.

"That's exactly what I think they are, but I'm awful glad to have someone else say the same thing. The other thing I've never heard of up on that land is any kind of cemetery. So not one thing about this is making sense to me."

Mark shook his head, resisting the urge to drop the horrible things on the couch cushion and go scrub his hands.

"I'm with you there. These don't look like animal teeth, either. Not with some of them dug out like they've had fillings. Have you taken them to a dentist, or maybe the police?"

"Sure did. Doc Copely agrees they're human, and not one of them with signs of modern dental work. Showed them to one of the deputies I know, too. I asked her about missing persons or unsolved murders and the like. Couldn't find anything worth investigating. They're not exactly set up for this kind of thing here in little old Boun County."

Mark stared up at the ceiling, made of strips of poplar just like the walls. He didn't want to get himself mixed up in whatever Art had uncovered, and he didn't want this assignment to end and force him back to Richmond too soon.

In about equal measures.

"I don't want to sound ungrateful," he said, "or like I don't want to help. But I'm not sure why you called DMME or asked for me, Art. I'm not set up for anything like forensics, either. Or for dealing with the kind of mess you have washing out in that creek."

Art glared at him for a few seconds, bushy black eyebrows shot through with gray drawn down level with his round glasses in a thunderous scowl. Then he shrugged, flashed a tight-lipped smile, and blushed all the way up to the fluff of his receding hairline.

"Well yeah, I know that. If I hadn't dealt so much with Mike Powell over the years and knew I could trust him, I would have lied through my teeth to get you instead of some random stranger with a fancy chemistry degree and not a clue about life back here in these mountains."

He drew in a long, deep breath and held it for several seconds before letting it out slow enough that Mark got antsy waiting.

"You remember how well I knew your Papaw Walt." He waited for Mark to nod. "He and my dad served together in the war in Germany, so I just about grew up with your own dad. I'm sure you remember how your Papaw had dreams sometimes. Or he called them dreams, but my father suspected he just said that because it sounded a tiny bit better than visions. Anyway, things about the past or what was coming down the pike."

Mark tried not to shiver, hearing Clina's voice echoing inside his mind, and quiet conversations with his Papaw through Clina and Beth.

And feeling that click, that certainty when Beth told him about Clina to begin with. He'd known he could believe

Beth because he'd grown up trusting and believing his Papaw.

He'd wondered himself if all of those *dreams* honestly involved what most people called sleep.

"We all knew to heed what Papaw told us either way," Mark said in a quiet voice. "'Cause he was never wrong."

"I never knew him to be wrong, either. I got the feeling he kept my dad safe more than once during the war, and kept me and your dad from our foolish notions more times than I care to admit. Now I never had anything as clear as dreams like he did, but I learned to trust my own hunches. My instinct, you might say, and I think that part of me got stronger because I *did* trust it."

He paused again, and Mark couldn't look away from the troubled, downright scared look he'd never seen in Art's eyes in all the years he'd known him.

"Mark, I'll admit to you and probably no one who didn't know your Papaw that I came all over goosebumps and terrible sick chills the instant my hands went in that water. The gloves couldn't block whatever's washing out of that mountain, and all the modern equipment and testing in this world would never detect it. But you'll never convince me as long as I live that something's not dangerous and wrong up there. Bad wrong."

Mark heard a raspy click in his own throat as he swallowed, and all his muscles locked rigid and cold. He hadn't felt that since the last dream his Papaw had ever told him about years ago, the last time the two of them talked in the middle of the night, victims of their shared trait of insomnia.

The dream of how and when he would die that had come true not two weeks later.

"That explains why Mr. Powell said a local boy needed to handle this," Mark said. "But I'm guessing you didn't tell him the whole story."

Art let out a grunting laugh, and Mark's tense body finally relaxed. A little.

"Hell no, I didn't tell him the whole thing. Just fibbed a little about how attached some of the locals are to that piece of land, even though I doubt anyone ever sets foot out there unless they have to. I'm not the only one who gets the creeps in that spot, but Mike doesn't know that. Maybe something about how they'd trust you to check it out, and be more inclined to listen to you about whatever had to be done."

Mark snorted out laughter himself.

"Set the bar a little higher, why don't you?"

Art smiled, but it didn't get anywhere within a mile of his eyes.

"Unless I really am losing it, the bar's set plenty high enough. I have to ask if this is something you're willing to take on. I'm not fibbing or lying or anything else when I say I'd understand if you're not. Whatever's up there half scared the life out of me. You ever feel that way about a place?"

This time Mark did shiver, and he didn't try to hide it. Maybe it was time he admitted at least a bit of what he and Beth (and Clina) had actually gotten into back in December.

"Just one time. When we were taking your lost miner's bones out of that old house pit. I was sure then and I'm more sure now that he dropped the rock that hit Beth on purpose. Thing is, I know in my bones that the rock was really aimed at me."

Mark didn't realize he'd brushed his fingers through the back of his hair—touching the spot where the rock likely would have landed—until Art glanced up, then looked back into Mark's eyes.

"My Granny taught me it's evil luck to mention such a thing out loud," Art said, "but Hartstown doesn't seem to be quite as cursed as it once was. I looked it up, you see. Since the awful day that school bus went into the river, we've seen a reduction in every kind of crime or accident or incident you can think up. Car crashes, fights, drunk driving. Domestic violence, workplace injuries, even emergency room and veterinarian visits. I don't know exactly what you and Beth did up there that day. Maybe you'll tell me sometime, over a beer or probably something stronger. All I do know is I don't want Hartstown to suffer like that again."

Mark nodded slowly, amazed at how the rational part of his brain locked onto the sensible thread he could follow. The drive and draw that had pushed him through high school and college and everything he'd learned and done since to clean up waterways and keep them clean.

Every other part of him teetered between awe and a breathy kind of shock.

Through it all, he couldn't wait to talk to Beth.

"You're worried this thing will go a lot farther than your creek. That it will make it all the way down to the river."

"Knew you'd catch on quick," Art said, slumping back against the couch. "We can keep our friends in Richmond happy, too, since there's something you can smell and test and measure. What do you say, Mark? You willing to get into this mess?"

Mark leaned back with a sigh of his own, closing his eyes.

He'd woken up less than twelve hours ago, in his ordinary and kind of boring bachelor apartment back in Richmond. Thinking of Beth as usual, and how every day he woke up without her felt like a letdown now. Hating that it would probably be a few more weeks before he made the drive to Hartstown.

He never could have imagined he'd be sitting here with Art Steffens of all people, one of the most practical and sensible folks Mark had ever known.

Or that he'd be wondering why Art had bothered asking,

even when the question seemed a million miles from the reality of that same morning.

"Of course I'm willing, Art. I noticed the change for the better in Hartstown, too. I'll do anything in my power to keep it that way."

Chapter 5

By the time Beth drove both of them to the grocery story
for provisions and on to her house, leaving Mark's official car
in town, he'd filled her in on everything Art said.

The hundred-year-old bungalow tucked against the
mountains on the edge of town was everything his Richmond apartment wasn't. Clearly loved and carefully tended
by the person who lived there. A person who felt settled, at
home. A person who meant to stay there for a good long
while.

Surrounded by towering oaks and maples older than the
house, with patches of flowers and garden boxes covering all
but a tiny bit of lawn right out front. All of it dormant and
bare except for arrangements of purple hyacinths and yellow,
pink, and white crocuses. Beth grumbled about having any
grass at all to waste space and take care of, but it hadn't irri-
tated her quite enough to rip the last bit of in-town
respectability out and replace it.

The house was painted a deep forest green that almost
blended in when the leaves were on thick and full, and the
broad and deep front porch and trim sported dark brown

that only increased the effect. Mark looked forward to days and nights warm enough to sit on the huge, thick-cushioned porch swing for hours with Beth, Janie curled up snoring at their feet on her own cushion softer and more comfortable than most human beds.

Inside more of the same mix of classic and comfortable waited, with gleaming hardwood floors and old-fashioned rag rugs, modern art prints and historical black and white photos on walls painted in soothing earth tones. Couches and chairs made for lounging and cuddling. A bedroom and even a huge bathtub made for so much more.

He'd been grateful for her skill of intense and silent listening while he was rushing to get it all out before he convinced *himself* he was crazy. Mark believed her claim of the habit coming from her years of journalism and inter-viewing people for the local history books she wrote.

But he strongly suspected part of it was simply the way she always observed—and absorbed—the world around her.

He'd talked himself out just as Beth parked in the short paved driveway leading up to her house. Now he was starting to itch for her to say something. Anything.

Beth gripped the steering wheel of her Maxima, cozy enough to have them almost shoulder to shoulder but big enough to leave Mark worried she would run inside, call the nearest mental health facility, and arrange for him and Art to take a nice, long "vacation."

"You think it could all start up again?" she said, her voice barely louder than the early evening breeze against the windows and the ticking engine. "If this thing gets to the river, Hartstown might drop right back into all the bad things happening?"

"I honestly don't know, Beth. I've known Art my whole life, and he's about the furthest person in the world from gullible or fanciful."

"Kind of like you and me." She ducked her head and smiled at him, then took his hand and squeezed harder than he expected. "But he grew up here and with folks from here."

"Kind of like you and me. I'm scared to death of what I might be walking into here, but I couldn't possibly turn away."

This time she turned in her seat to face him. "What *you're* walking into? Think you'd walk into anything like this alone, do you?"

"I know you don't want to hear this, especially from me. But maybe we should let your arm finish healing up before you go charging into another cave."

Beth rolled her eyes and gave out her half sigh, half growl. Mark's earlier amorous response was tempered by worry for her. She let go of his hand and touched the copper shining at her throat.

"Okay then, what does Clina think?" he said, resisting the urge to reach for her hand again so he could hear for himself. "Or my Papaw?"

She shook her head, staring out the window and away from him.

"You think if one of them tells me to settle down and stay out of the way, I'll listen?"

Mark closed his eyes for a second, not sure how to dig himself out of the hole he was in.

"I know you don't need permission from them or me or anyone else. But I didn't much care for you getting hurt. Even though you were keeping me from getting hurt worse."

She glanced at him, then looked away again.

"There are moments," she said, "not very often or for very long, but moments when I wonder if I should have let that rock fall on your head."

He took a chance and touched her shoulder, just above where the fracture had finally healed.

"I'm sure you'll feel that way a lot more often the longer you know me."

Beth leaned back into his touch for a few seconds before she turned and hugged him tight.

"I'm going with you, Mark. That's the end of it. Clina and your Papaw think we might all be able to figure this out. If we work together."

Mark nodded, his lips against her hair, breathing in her citrus shampoo and a deeper scent that was all her. The breeze outside was picking up steam, matching the low clouds that had finally arrived.

"Okay," he said. "We work together. Let's get inside before it gets too cold. Janie will never forgive me if she figures out I waited out here instead of dashing in to say hello."

Chapter 6

MARK OPENED his eyes in the dark, wide awake after sleeping like the dead.

The distant, melancholy call of a train whistle sounded again.

He didn't want to move enough to get his watch off the nightstand. Knowing exactly the hour of his current bout of insomnia wasn't worth waking Beth on his right side, or disturbing Janie and her soft hound dog snores on his left.

Early supper and early lovemaking had combined with the stresses and surprises of the day to put him out long before his usual bedtime. He'd known from years of experience that he'd never sleep through the night. But the intensity and release of the best sex he'd ever had with Beth or anyone else sent him off anyway.

Mark hadn't realized how much he'd been holding back, how careful he'd been of Beth's arm. Maybe how guilty he'd felt about her being hurt. Hurt because of him no matter how he sliced it.

He'd had no idea Beth was holding back so much of herself, either.

But tonight, they'd both shed any caution or restraint. Between that and getting over the closest they'd ever come to a fight, the results had been spectacular.

Mind-blowing if he was being honest, which he almost always managed awake with his thoughts in the middle of the night.

Quick little pleasure aftershocks sparked through his body and mind at the memory.

Much as he wanted to stay right there and store up the sensations for lonely weeks without her, his too-alert mind dragged him back to the reason he was in Hartstown to begin with.

Art's creek and whatever was going on up there that had everyone—including Mark—so spooked.

Because as it had done since he was a teenager, Mark's brain insisted the best way to pass the hours between bedtime and sunrise would be to obsess over things he couldn't do the slightest damn thing about right now.

He shifted onto his other side, getting a mumbling turn from Beth and a series of grunts and long sighs from Janie. Finally they all settled with Janie curled up warm against Mark's back and him curled up against Beth's. Anyone else in the world should have dropped right back off.

Test results and topo maps scrolled behind his closed eyes instead. That and the unusual fear in Art's eyes.

Something dangerous and wrong. *Bad* wrong.

Mark raised up enough to reach toward Beth's nightstand. If he couldn't get to his own watch, maybe he could grab hers for a quick time check.

He jerked his hand back when a low, muttering voice jumped into his mind.

The miner they'd rescued, talking a blue streak just like Papaw said all those weeks ago. Mark still couldn't understand the words, but the man's distinctive deep voice sounded about a thousand times more calm. Less lonesome. He was conversing now, rather than moaning and crying for anyone to please hear him, please listen. Desperate attempts to get one single soul on the face of the earth, or under it, to admit that he'd ever been alive.

Did that mean Mark's grandfather was there, close by and paying the attention the lost miner so badly needed? Papaw had shared Mark's insomniac night owl tendencies. They'd met many a time wandering around Mark's grandparents' house, hunting for a book, heading down to raid the kitchen. Sitting on the porch swing staring out at the mountains under the full moon or the blackest quiet night.

If he could manage to talk softly enough to keep from waking Beth—and from drawing further disapproval from Janie—this might be a fine time for a chat.

Assuming Clina would agree. She seemed to be the gatekeeper to what Beth called the radio station inside her head. At the very least, Clina was the key.

Mark took a deep breath, leaned forward again, and slowly twined the chain around his fingers, not touching the bit of glass yet. His stubborn wide-awake mind brought it into spotlit and magnified hyper-clear focus.

He'd only seen the full glass plate negative once before it shattered itself—their miner's last victim. Instead of a group of mourners on a black and white hillside, all dressed in their best for a turn-of-the-last-century funeral, now the only image was of a woman's face. Mark knew this was probably the only surviving picture of Clina Jane, dark-haired with a huge white hat perched at a strangely jaunty angle on her head. He had no idea of her last name.

A buddy of his back in Richmond had smoothed the jagged glass edges just enough to remove any razor blade bits, sealed the whole thing to protect it, and coated the sides in a thick, solid layer of copper.

Beth loved the result even more than Mark hoped. But he understood why she took the necklace off before they made love, and before she went to sleep every night. To get a bit of peace and quiet inside her own head.

Clina could still get through if she tried, and the singing and music all around her floated through from time to time. Without the constant chatter and higher volume the necklace brought, Beth had figured out how to turn it all down to background noise so she could get back to her normal sound, deep sleep.

Mark envied her that easy lifelong ability. People who slept well never quite seemed to understand how good they had it.

He settled back into his warm nest between his two favorite nighttime companions, awake or asleep. No worries about losing physical contact with Beth in her snug, comfortable bed. As long as he could keep his voice low enough, everything should be just fine.

Unless Clina decided to let Beth know he'd been chatting through her while he excluded her in the middle of the night.

"File under 'I'll deal with it tomorrow,'" he whispered. He turned his wrist so the glass with Clina's century-old photo rested in his palm.

Silence.

Neither the miner or anyone else made a sound, but Mark heard that open channel hum Beth talked about. Even if no one was currently broadcasting, the station was online.

Or maybe it was alive.

Mark dropped his voice lower than a whisper, only the slightest breath of air passing through his throat.

"Papaw? Are you there?"

He counted his heartbeats, doing his best to brace himself so he wouldn't jump. It worked about as well as it always did, which was to say not at all.

A voice raspy from what the old man always called his rough-living youth spoke up inside Mark's head, the rise and fall of the words a song in his heart.

"Hey there water bug. What you doin' up so late?"

Mark smiled at the nickname he'd earned before he even started school. No one had ever managed to keep him out of puddles, creeks, rivers, you name it. With Papaw's encouragement, they'd given up at last and encouraged him instead.

"Hey yourself, mud bug. Same thing you are, I reckon. Waiting for the sun to come up."

A gruff chuckle floated through the quiet.

"Seems you outgrew that about as well as I did. Got something on your mind, or is your mind just rambling?"

"All kinds of things on my mind, Papaw. Anybody else up where you are?"

"Well, to tell you the truth, we're all pretty much up, or at least wakeful. That whole eternal rest nonsense turned out to be a long ways from the truth, but I guess that's okay. We still get more peace and quiet at night than a lot of folks. So you don't get to feeling shy, Clina Jane stepped away for a bit so we could catch up. Took over listening to our new buddy for a while. That boy sure can talk a blue streak."

"Sounds like me when I was a kid. What's his name, Papaw? I just realized I never heard anyone say it."

Another pause, and Mark concentrated on Beth and Janie. Both of them slumbered on.

He wondered for a second if Beth was dreaming this conversation.

"Nearest I can say is Dusanek," his Papaw said. Du-*sah*-neck. "We're getting better at working out what the other's trying to get across. You never did say what's got you fretting, Mark. I don't think it's trouble with your Beth, not to hear Clina tell the tale. But I hear trouble in your voice, just like I always did."

"Yeah, I figured you might. It's work stuff, partly. Cleaning up water and trying to keep it that way. But there's something more going on here. Something I don't understand."

"Go ahead and talk it all out if you want to, water bug. I always had time for you, if you remember. Now I got all the time in your world and the next."

Mark blinked back tears, trying to keep countless memories from covering him up in a mostly happy flood. He and his parents had settled into a friendly enough pattern over the years. But he knew as well as they did that they'd never quite understood each other. Beth seemed to have about the same loving but slightly puzzled relationship with her folks.

Not much had ever soothed Mark's restless mind like talking to his Papaw, at least not until he met the woman sleeping beside him.

So, he talked it all out.

His Papaw was silent when he finished, and Mark could so clearly see him scratching at his chin, then looking up under his bushy eyebrows while he gathered his thoughts. Right on cue, he started talking.

"I sure understand why that's got you upset, Mark. And why it's got Art tore to pieces. With both of you saying something's wrong, anyone with any sense would pay attention. That land was out along old Route 43, you say?"

"That's it. About five miles away from where I am now."

"Okay. I'll do some asking around, but I'd just about swear I heard tales about that place when I was young. Not young like you are, but just a school boy. I'd say Art knows who owned it and when, or could find out over at the courthouse."

Mark sighed, sleepy tendrils blooming in his head, reaching out to his arms and chest and legs. His mind might finally be convinced to slow down enough so he could join Beth and Janie.

"That would be a huge help, Papaw. I'm afraid I'm going to need all the help anyone's willing to give me on this one."

"I want you to be careful, now. When you get a bad feeling like this, you got to heed it."

"I sure will, don't worry. I don't want anything bad to happen now that I'm finally getting my life together, you know?"

That chuckle again, rough and raspy and sounding every bit as comforting and safe as it had since Mark was that muddy little water bug toddler.

"I'm awful glad to hear that. Now go get some sleep if you can. All your troubles will still be waiting for you when you wake."

"I will. Thank you, Papaw."

Mark yawned as he leaned forward to let the necklace drop into place where he'd found it.

Art had indeed given him a thick folder he was pretty sure had copies of all the deeds that had ever been attached to that land. He'd been too distracted to look at them once he and Beth got home.

Strangely for him, he wasn't willing to move a single inch to go look at them now, even though his mind could have happily perked right back up and focused until the sun rose over the mountains. The routine he knew as well as the Boun County roads they'd be driving in a few hours.

Maybe because even though he was still a guest in Beth's house and he'd return to his own apartment (whether he wanted to or not), every part of him knew he was indeed home.

In this bed, with his arms around her. Warmed by her body, listening to her breathe.

With a dreaming redbone hound dog twitching against his back.

Home.

Before he could count to five, Mark was sound asleep.

Chapter 7

THE ROAD out to Art's current troublesome plot of land was thankfully much smoother and easier than the rutted old mining road they'd taken months ago. Mark had manfully refused Beth's offer to borrow her brother's tank of a pickup truck again. So he was greatly relieved that yesterday's clouds still lingered but had dropped neither snow nor rain, and that his work sedan made the trip with no problems at all.

Neither of them pointed out that even someone spoiled by city driving for a decade could manage the twisty but well-maintained gravel bed Art always had installed after one of his big land buyouts.

The mountains around them still showed recent scars of clear-cutting, a water problem Mark hated but had never been able to focus on. A few straggly stumps poked up here or there, along with low scrubby plants that had barely managed to get a foothold before last winter set in.

But the slope rising up beside their narrow parking spot was stripped bare of the towering oaks, poplars, maples, and pines that provided the texture and beauty to the land only a couple of years before.

He knew Art and his dedicated crew of tree-planters would get going a bit later in the spring, and that their efforts over the next few years would turn this spot into a green and healthy oasis someday. In another lifetime or two.

For now, Mark was faced with desolation every bit as awful as the black and white photos Beth had shown him at the town hall. Records of the ruins left by Boun County's original slash-and-run timber barons.

Even deeper scars crisscrossed the landscape now, the bare and flattened earth marking mechanical haul-out paths for all that timber, valuable or not.

That was what Mark hated most, and Beth's scowl and compressed lips told him she felt the same. He understood harvesting wood, even majestic old hardwoods. Trees were renewable, after all, and nothing could come close to the look and feel of a fine piece of woodworking.

Ripping everything down in the name of a faster, cheaper harvest turned his stomach.

Not quite as badly as the fast runoff of gunk left by all those saws and equipment, and of soil that couldn't hang on where it belonged anymore. With no healthy undergrowth or leaves overhead to slow rain or snowmelt down—and no effort to withdraw gracefully by what he suspected was a repeat offender tree harvesting outfit—the torrent was set free to foul every tributary and waterway all the way to the Mississippi or the Atlantic.

Art was right about the mess out here. Mark had never seen a timber operation so badly managed outside of Beth's photographs.

The creek beside his car ran brown and sludgy, making every effort to prove his point.

Beth slipped her cold hand into his, reminding him they weren't out there because of typical pollution, if there was such a thing. Mark took a deep breath and caught only an earthy, mineral scent. Closer to a healthy river at natural flood stage than anything chemical.

Or sinister.

He wasn't sure, but he thought she might be wearing the same faded blue and red flannel shirt as on their previous adventure. He wore his own faded Tech t-shirt, plucked out of their jumble of discarded clothing that morning.

He wasn't much of a believer in luck, good or bad. But he hoped thinking of all the good that had come out of their encounter with the lost miner—for them and for all of Hartstown—would overwhelm the bad of this place. And quiet his own fear.

Mark lowered his face toward the open collar of his own flannel shirt and breathed in Beth's scent.

Maybe a bit of good luck wasn't a bad idea after all.

"Where did Art say the polluted stream is?" she said, staring up at the desolate land.

Maps inside his head shifted and aligned with everything he'd heard yesterday. He pointed just to the left, where the swell of a hill was barely visible behind two others.

"He didn't get too far, not far enough to see the headwaters for his bad stream. Depends on how the footing is where the creeks run. We may have to cover some steep, muddy ground to get to the source if they're too nasty."

She smirked and raised one eyebrow at him.

"Steep I can handle. You sure you're up for it, city boy?"

"I reckon I can manage if you go easy on me."

Mark kissed her cheek and grabbed their backpacks out of the trunk. He'd packed his small respirators in an abundance of caution, or maybe paranoia. The waterproof gloves seemed a lot more important after the testing results and Art's description.

The old land records showed no evidence of mining, nor any kind of homesteading that might have left an unlisted house pit. As far as Mark or Art or anyone at the Boun County courthouse knew, this land hadn't been much except part of one of the original parcels held by Reginald Hart. His efforts to develop the area and carve Boun County out of the sprawling old governing divisions a hundred and fifty years ago got the new county seat named after him. But that was about all anyone knew about him.

No one had much bothered with this spot, apparently not even for hunting, from the first time it was clear-cut back in the 1800s. Not until the trees were again stripped bare last year.

Beth took the pickaxe, smiling as she hefted it in her right hand. Mark pretended not to notice how fast her hand dropped and started shaking before she transferred it to her left.

He in turn appreciated her ignoring his frown when he clipped his ancient, trusty machete onto his belt. Probably not much need for it when nothing yet grew higher than his thighs, but the habit of almost thirty years had worn a groove in his brain.

"Any advice from Clina?" Mark said, a newer habit he'd gotten into with Beth.

Too late, he realized he hadn't mentioned his late-night talk with his grandfather to her.

He truly *had* meant to that morning, before both of them woke with other ideas in mind. Not quite as spectacular as the night before, but more than enough to pleasantly addle his thought processes. Then coffee and breakfast and Art's folders and maps pushed his confession right off his inner to-do list.

"Just that we're to mind her and your Papaw and everyone else wherever they are and be careful." She glanced at him, with a frown and scowl of her own. "Your Papaw says he's still asking around about those stories he heard? When he was a little boy?"

Mark looked down, surprised and a little embarrassed to see he was kicking at the bright new gravels under their feet.

No different than when he'd gotten caught out as a little boy. His face was turning red to complete the effect.

"I'm sorry, Beth. I couldn't sleep last night, and I reached for your watch to see what time it was. I didn't want to wake Janie reaching for mine. I accidently brushed your necklace, and… Well, I talked to Papaw for a while. He had insomnia as bad as I do, so we used to talk all the time while everyone else was asleep. I just didn't think."

He risked a peek at her, not wanting to look any more like a kid than he had to. Her forehead was still wrinkled, but she seemed to be fighting off a smile.

"You reached over me instead of Janie? So you wouldn't wake her?"

"I did," Mark said. Now he was trying not to smile himself. "Believe me, now that I said it out loud I hear exactly how weird that sounds."

She looked away again, but Mark caught her grin.

"Can you at least tell me you two didn't talk *about* me while I was asleep?"

"I promise, we did not talk about you. He'll back me up on that. To tell you the truth, I ran my mouth about myself and worrying about whatever we're walking into right now." Mark leaned closer, his lips only a couple of inches from her ear. "I do know Papaw likes you."

Beth snorted and turned to face him. Her lips were pressed tight again, but the upward curve and the sparkle in her eyes gave everything away.

"But does he like me better than Janie? Don't forget I'm holding a pickaxe."

Mark laughed and reached for her free hand. She swatted him away before she linked her fingers through his.

"He likes you better than Janie," Mark said. "But he hasn't had a chance to speak to Janie yet."

She rolled her eyes and shook her head before she laughed under her breath.

"Okay, smartass. Maybe we can talk about this tonight. Set up a few ground rules before the next time you decide to use me as some kind of radio transmitter. In case you were wondering, you didn't wake me up."

Mark kissed her cheek again.

"Well good. There's one mission accomplished, anyway. I really am sorry, Beth."

She stared at him for several seconds. "I didn't know you had so much trouble sleeping. You must hide it well. We might be able to work something out with your Papaw if it lets you rest easier."

Mark tried not to shiver, without much success. "I'd like that. Assuming whatever's out here doesn't give us both nightmares."

He'd shown Beth the disturbing handful of what he and Art and Doc Copely were certain were teeth that morning. The two of them had promptly zipped the disturbing things up in a plastic baggie, then locked them in the sedan's trunk.

Neither of them wanted to touch the horrible remnants, though neither of them had been bothered by handling the miner's bones back in December.

Something about the teeth—more so than anything Mark had ever found underground or anywhere else—left him shuddering inside. Sometimes outside.

He despised the idea of Beth being threatened by or even exposed to whatever was happening out here on Art's land. Even though she'd saved *his* life back in that house pit, he still felt the same.

And despite his fit of feeling like a kid caught with his hand in the cookie jar, he was old enough to know when arguing was going to cause more harm than good.

Hand in hand, heavy ballast gravel along the edge of the road crackling and shifting under their feet, Beth and Mark headed out.

They smelled trouble before they saw it.

Chapter 8

The walk turned out easier than Mark expected, with the creek that flowed between the hills running calm and low. Not quite as thick and sluggish as back by the car, but with that same muddy, flood-stage smell.

At first.

The almost bare land rising around them showed countless ridges and grooves from runoff. The heavy winter snow had to have taken a toll, along with unusual cold. Many of the puddles around the edges of the creek glistened with a rainbow sheen and smelled faintly of gas and oil.

A proper cleanup of the whole site would be well worth the time and effort, assuming Mark and Art together could secure the funding.

Scrubby plants grew beside and into the flowing water, the floating varieties green and pliant and gearing up for new growth. He hadn't walked this part of Boun County before, but Mark could so clearly imagine what the mossy contours along the creek would have been like while the trees were still there. Shady and cool, smelling fresh and green.

But whatever he was smelling now was anything but fresh.

He glanced at Beth, who was already wrinkling her nose.

"What *is* that?" she said.

Mark was surprised the gray and white and green pebbles and rocks in the water (no teeth so far) didn't have a yellowish tint from the heavy sulfurous aroma.

"Like the gates of hell, isn't it? Hydrogen sulfide."

She shook her head, dropping his hand so she could cover her nose. "I know rotten egg gas when I smell it. This is different. Worse."

He breathed in again, and this time his whole body tried to recoil away from the air itself. Not sulfur, or at least not that by itself. A hint of…well, ammonia, like the stink of an overused litter box. And an overheated chemical smell, like burning plastic.

Mark covered his own nose then, admitting Beth was right about worse. So much worse.

It wasn't only the smell, though that was bad enough.

The air *felt* wrong. Oily and heavy, cold and sticky against his skin.

His sinuses and lungs seemed to clench inside him. Maybe telling him he shouldn't be exposing them to the horrible atmosphere around him.

He reached for his backpack and the clear plastic half-face respirators that didn't seem the least bit paranoid now.

"I don't know how much these will help with that stench," he said, handing one to Beth.

"I don't care." She dropped the pickaxe and grabbed for it. "I'm going to choke to death."

He couldn't argue. He was too busy pulling his own respirator on, trying to fit it before his throat closed up. Countless airline safety video admonitions to secure his own mask before helping others forced him to take his time before he held Beth's steady and adjusted the straps.

The stink dropped to tolerable levels, and the panicky feeling eased in his chest.

"I don't know how the hell Art walked farther than this with no protection," he said, looking at the pebbles along the streambed ahead of them. Still nothing unusual.

"Maybe it got worse after he was here."

Beth rubbed at her hands and face, clearly feeling the awfulness of the air around them. She reached for the copper chain around her neck the instant Mark wondered if she should.

"Clina?" she said. "Everything looks normal, but it feels like we're walking into a wall of solid evil out here."

He took Beth's outstretched hand.

"…don't know for sure what's hitting you right now," Clina was saying. "But I've heard tell of such things many times before. This ain't like our miner you helped bring home to us. He was crying his broken heart out trying pull souls down under the earth with him. Could be the place itself is bad."

"It seems to be getting worse," Mark said, looking into Beth's eyes. "I hadn't heard anything about this spot before. From what our friend told me, no one likes to be out here. He also said it didn't feel this bad just a few days ago."

"Something might have got disturbed," Clina said. "Like a drafty wind blowing a fire up too high if you don't watch it." She paused, and Mark heard muttering in the background. No music like he'd heard before, but a lot of voices. "Now heed what I say, both of you. You might be caught up in the middle of land that got spoiled. Sounds strange, but sometimes the truth hits a body that way. Or could be bad things happened that left a scar down deep in the land."

Mark looked around at the cracked and muddy brown

earth, the stubble of trees and brush that would need at least twenty years to recover. He knew that wasn't the kind of scar Clina was talking about.

"We might want to go back," he said, still holding Beth's hand. "At least get better equipment. Maybe check at the town hall or the courthouse, see what we can find."

Beth stared at him, her blue eyes flashing. In his mind he saw her just as clearly, glaring at him in the faint glow of their flashlights in middle of the miner's pit. Those same beautiful eyes tight with pain and fear after that rock broke her arm.

Telling him they couldn't back out now and hope things didn't get worse.

This time, she only nodded and grabbed the pickaxe.

"Clina," she said as they turned and started walking, "Mark's Papaw was going to ask around, see if anyone there remembered trouble out here. Do you know if he found anything?"

"He's been chattering up a storm, catching anyone who sits still long enough. Don't think he's found out a thing. Not yet."

Mark watched the ground beneath their feet, trying to remember where the air was last clear and clean. What he drew into his lungs even through the respirator still felt foul and choking, and his hands, face, and neck still felt coated with cold, gummy filth. That could be air still trapped in the filter. And his skin would scrub clean as soon as he could get to soap and scalding hot water.

The truth was he needed to draw in a fresh breath badly enough to risk it.

He eased the respirator down and sniffed, seeing Beth do the same.

She coughed and cried out, but Mark was too busy coughing to help.

"It's worse!" she said once she covered her nose and mouth again. "How could it be so much *worse?*"

Mark shook his head and wiped at his streaming eyes.

"It shouldn't be. See those footprints in the mud? That twist of rock in the middle? I remember that. The air was clear here when we walked in. Not even ten minutes ago."

Beth grabbed for his hand again.

"It's moving, Clina. Not just the water, but the air. Whatever's wrong is spreading, and fast."

Silence, long enough for Beth to lean the pickaxe against her leg and catch Mark's other hand.

"Not a one of us can hear a thing where you are, Beth. I can't get ahold of what you're after."

"What's after *us* now," Mark said.

"That might just be the truth," Clina said, and her worried voice ratcheted Mark's nerves a bit tighter. "What we don't rightly know is how long you can wait. Has this thing hurt anyone? In the body?"

Beth raised her eyebrows and shrugged.

"We haven't heard of anything like that," she said. "But we haven't had a good chance to look yet. You think if no one's been hurt, we'll be okay to check it out?"

Another pause, leaving every cell in Mark's body wanting to get them both back to the car and out of there. He didn't know who the hell he would call to come in as backup or what kind of equipment might actually protect them, but he was willing to give it a good try.

"Ain't neither one of you hurt right now?" Clina said. "Best give me the truth, not some kind of nonsense like to get you both killed."

"We're both fine," Beth said. "The air's hard to breathe, but we have help with that."

"Then I reckon you could go on," Clina said slowly. "If you can work out what this thing is, might be able to keep it from getting worse. Either one of you touch anything? Carry anything out of there?"

Mark grunted, wishing he could give a different answer.

"We didn't, but our friend did. He brought out something he found in the creek here. Not here, really, a good bit farther up."

Clina's sigh was so long and clear Mark looked at Beth to see if she'd done it. She only shook her head and winked.

"You mean to ask me for my help and not tell me what got toted out of there? Exactly how do you think I'm supposed to figure anything out that way?"

"Okay," Mark said, once again feeling like a little boy in for a well-deserved scolding. "But remember, you did ask. Art found what he thinks are teeth, mixed in with all the pebbles on the stream bed. Human teeth. The roots are broken off, but they look like teeth to me, too."

"I think they're right," Beth said, shuddering. "Teeth. They made me feel bad when I touched them. Kind of like the air here is now."

Mark heard more of that low level muttering before Clina answered. He was indescribably glad a whole group of people were trying to help them, ghosts or not.

"We still don't rightly know if you got a bad place or a bad person. But I think it's a fair guess whatever it is got stirred up by your friend carrying those teeth away. You got 'em with you now?"

"Down in my car," Mark said. "A few minutes walk down and back."

"We were afraid having them with us would make things worse," Beth said. "You think we need to get them?"

"I'm real sorry, Beth," Clina said, her voice unusually soft and gentle. "I sure don't know what to tell you on that. Wish I did. You and Mark got to trust your gut."

Beth stared into Mark's eyes, her eyebrows raised. She

held his hands so tightly his knuckles were starting to hurt, but he didn't dare shift or let go.

"I hope this doesn't sound as crazy as I feel," Mark said. "But I think we should bring them back up here. I can't think of a single fairy tale or legend or anything else when taking something away didn't mean you had to bring it right back."

"Makes as much sense to me as any of this," Beth said. "Maybe we can mark where the smell is on the way down."

Mark wished with all his heart he could think of something positive or optimistic to say. But a situation like this seemed to call for honesty more than anything else.

"Assuming whatever it is doesn't follow us all the way to the car."

Chapter 9

ALL THE WAY to the car was still a safe zone, though Mark wasn't sure it would last much longer. By the time he and Beth got the horrible teeth and hiked back up, the miasma had rolled at least another fifty yards down the creek bed.

The only positive thing they could grab onto was once they crossed the stink line, it didn't seem to get thicker the farther they walked.

They made it past their own muddy footprints before things managed to get worse.

Beth grabbed Mark's arm and pulled him to a stop.

"Did Art mention anything like that?"

He followed where she pointed with the pickaxe and gasped, or as close as he could to it with the respirator on. Rather than the flat green of last year's growth or the fragile, pale green of new spring life, the plants in and around the water were dead white.

No, not dead. None of them seemed to be the least bit unhealthy. The ferns, moss, vines, even a few spots of hair-like algae caught against big rocks and wavering in the water appeared to have full summertime vigor. Firm and plump, not at all withered or wilted.

Mark stepped closer, glad he had several more plastic zip-top bags in his backpack, and even more glad he had waterproof gloves. He wanted these bizarre things analyzed as soon as he could get them back to Richmond.

"Art didn't say a word about this," Mark said. He squatted over a patch of moss along the creek bed, bigger than his hands put together and in perfect moist and spongy condition. Other than looking more like a fresh coat of snow than any kind of local growth. "I heard of a white moss a long time ago, but it grows way north of here. As in around the Yukon north. This is regular old sheet moss for right where we are. But what we walked over on the way up here was dark green."

He looked downstream, where only a few yards away the natural color resumed.

"Doesn't smell anything like our moss, either," he said. "As far as white plants, we get ghost pipe, Papaw called it corpse plant, but usually not out in the open like this. Those don't even use chlorophyll. They get their energy from trees and fungus, but all the trees are gone. These look too healthy for this time of year to be starving. What the hell are they *eating*?"

Beth put her hands on his back and leaned forward, staring into the creek. The water still ran a little bit cloudy, but clear enough to see the usual pebbles at the bottom. Even with the stink and horrible feel of the air all around them, the normal, cheery burbling music of the creek that broke the quiet was reassuring.

"Speaking of eating, no signs of teeth so far," she said. "Thank goodness. How far did Art walk?"

Mark stood and turned in a circle, letting the contours of

the nearly bare mountains arrange themselves against the maps in his mind.

"I'd say another half mile or so. You doing okay?"

She laughed and shook her head. "Besides this horrible smell? And the moss and plants I've seen my whole life managing to lose all of their color? I'm okay. My arm and shoulder are a little achy, but I'll do."

A muffled crack sounded off to the left, something like the snap of a breaking branch. They both jerked that way, but nothing was visible around the curve of the hillside.

"I know I shouldn't mention things like this out loud," Mark said. "But we don't have any idea if whatever we're chasing affects animals."

"Or *how* it affects them," Beth said. She reached for her necklace and Mark's hand at the same time. "Anyone picking up on what's in front of us, Clina? Or find those stories about this land? Something's wrong with the plants along the water. They're turning white."

Instead of Clina's high pitched and usually smartass voice, they heard the raspy tones of Mark's Papaw.

"Hey there Beth, Mark. Think I might have a clue to what's happening there where you're headed to. Not sure about how to fix it just yet, but we'll figure that out as we go."

Mark watched Beth, wondering if she'd feel as instantly reassured by the words and even the voice as he did. He probably would have balked at anyone else in the world saying they'd figure something this strange out as they went.

Anyone besides his Papaw, and Beth.

"That sounds like progress to me," she said, walking forward and bringing Mark with her. "What did you find?"

"Well, this place is right crowded," Papaw said. "More than you'd think, even though not everyone finds their way to us. Not even everyone who passes over in Boun County.

But I asked around enough until I found the first one to own the land you're standing on right now. First to own it in the way we mean with deeds and all, I guess I should say."

Mark nodded, too busy looking around for whatever made the noise as they walked to realize his Papaw couldn't see him for several seconds.

"Who'd you find, Papaw? Mr. Hart?"

Beth shook her head with a crooked little smile.

"Naaah, wasn't him that started things up in Boun County," Papaw said. "Though he sure was happy to take the credit for it all. I been talking to Mr. Zachary Boun."

When Mark focused on Beth, she nodded.

"That's one of the county's dirty little secrets I came across in the town hall and the courthouse. Clina Jane got me in the habit of comparing records between the two, and it's been great for the book. I haven't decided if I'm going to put the controversy between Mr. Hart and Mr. Boun in yet."

"You best put that in!" Clina snapped. "You dug it out and a bunch of us here told you it's the plain truth. Now your man's Papaw managed to track down one of the men who was there, so there ain't no reason to go along with the nonsense that's been peddled all these years."

Beth grinned, even though she was as busy searching for the noise-maker as Mark.

"Hang on a second," Mark said. "I've heard my whole life that Reginald Hart did the founding around here."

Chapter 10

Beth stepped across a wide spot in the creek, letting go of Mark's hand to get her balance. The white discoloration continued along the waterway. And worse, it was spreading into the grasses and scrubby brush alongside. The bigger plants looked just as healthy and vigorous as the moss and algae, except for all the leaves and branches.

Still no sign of whatever had made that snapping noise, but they kept walking. No sound at all except their footsteps and the quiet mutter of the creek.

"That's what they taught us in school," Beth said, catching Mark's hand again when he stepped across. "All about Mr. Hart and all his civic pride and ambition and sacrifice. That's what's in all the old newspapers, too. But a few of the very oldest records buried in the town hall say otherwise. Some of the land records in the courthouse, too. The big old books that got caught in more than one flood, so they're kind of hard to handle if you're bothered by mold and mildew. Which I am, by the way."

Mark tried not to roll his eyes at the various ways he never would have imagined any of this just twenty-four hours ago. Or at the way his Papaw and Clina and a bunch of other fool ghosts laughed at Beth's words.

"Then maybe you can take me with you next time," he said. "So I'll have some idea what on earth you're talking about in the future."

"I'll do that," Beth said. "From what I can tell, the two of them knew each other when this was still part of Washington County. Partners in a few business ventures and land speculation deals. They had some kind of falling out, then Mr. Boun disappeared. Mr. Hart got a whole lot more prominent in the county's history after that."

"Then I guess we should hear what Mr. Boun has to—"

Three much louder cracks rang out, this time from somewhere up ahead. Not quite sharp enough to be gunshots, but close enough that both Mark and Beth stopped and crouched in place.

The creek curved abruptly to the left around a couple of boulders taller than Mark, hiding whatever could be making the noise. A cluster of small oak trees—apparently too young and close to the water for the loggers to deal with—huddled on the far side in front of the boulders.

Somehow the deathly white hue of the wrinkly bark, thin branches, and even the leaf buds scared Mark more than whatever the hell was waiting for them.

"That sounded like rocks," Beth whispered. "I thought it was a branch before."

"Yeah, me too. Any chance you'll stay behind me?"

She gripped his hand more tightly and glanced at him, flashing a quick smile.

"Why? Because of all your experience with mysterious crackling rock noises on clear cut sites in the middle of nowhere?"

A new voice cut through, so clear that Mark wondered if the speaker waited around that bend.

"You want to be careful, right there where you are. Not far past that spot turned out to be the end of me."

"Mr. Boun," Beth said, straightening out of her crouch. "Unless you can help us deal with whatever is around the corner, we may have to talk to you once we get out of here."

"I surely do wish you'd listen to me now."

His voice was soft and higher pitched than Mark would have expected. His mind always read and heard famous men's voices as deep and resonant, a bit like James Earl Jones.

"We can hear you," Mark said. "Tell me what we're walking into."

"The teeth." Beth stepped forward. "Mark, the teeth."

Caught in an eddy along one of the oak tree's bright white roots, a cluster of the same kind of yellowish, worn teeth Art collected were visible under the surface.

The teeth Mark now had in his backpack.

He hoped his own voice wasn't too shaky, that he wasn't transmitting how fast and hard his heart was beating.

"Want to tell us anything about the teeth in the creek bed, Mr. Boun?"

"Or the cracking noises we keep hearing?" Beth said.

"You got two great big rocks in front of you?" Mr. Boun said. "Right along Scatterland Creek? Probably the biggest trees you ever saw growed up around it now. Couldn't hardly see the tops of the giant chestnuts when I was last breathing."

A stab of sadness cut right through the fear in Mark's belly, and he closed his watering eyes for a second. He'd seen image after image of the massive chestnut trees that covered this part of the Appalachian Mountains before the blight, some approaching giant sequoias on the West Coast in girth and jaw-dropping height.

All fallen a hundred years ago to disease and saw.

Mark wished he could have seen those incredible forests more often than he cared to admit.

Beth looked every bit as stricken and upset. After all, she'd been the one to show Mark the old black and white photos.

"We made it through those beautiful trees, sir," Mark said, squeezing Beth's hand. "Right up the creek bed. Scatterland Creek. We're in front of those rocks, and it sounds like something a little farther along isn't exactly happy to see us."

Mr. Boun's voice dropped then, and he sounded as frightened as Mark felt.

"Nothing in that spot was ever what you might call happy. No person that I know of that stayed there for long got back to happy in their life, neither. That's if they had what you could call life left. You say you see teeth there, Miss Beth? You got past those two big rocks, then."

"Well, no, sir. Not yet. We're still behind them. The teeth are down in the water, along the creek bed. There's a horrible smell and feel to the air, too."

Mark heard a gasp, and Beth's raised eyebrows showed she'd heard it as well.

"That thing's done broke open," Mr. Boun said, his words low and shuddering. "Spilling all that pizen out into the world."

"Pizen," Beth whispered, her eyes wide and afraid now.

Mark's mind flashed back to a couple of days after their adventure in the miner's old house pit, when Beth was really starting to realize how long she'd have to deal with the cast on her arm.

And he was starting to realize how hard he was falling for her.

She'd told him everything she remembered about how the whole thing started, including Clina using that old dialect for poison.

He reached back to smooth the hackles standing up on the back of his neck and made the unpleasant discovery that the gummy air had settled into his hair as much as onto his skin.

"What can we do about it?" Mark said.

He raised his eyebrows and jerked his chin toward the bend in the creek. He truly didn't want to get closer, but the idea of standing around in some kind of poison longer than they had to—supernatural or not—wasn't sitting well with him, either.

Beth took a deep breath through her respirator, shrugged, and nodded.

They walked forward, holding onto the disturbing dead white oaks to keep their boots out of the water.

"No one ever did try to stop it," Mr. Boun said, "not while I was living. Couldn't work out how. Best thing is to get yourself away from there, and *stay* away."

Mark managed to work himself in front of Beth by twisting his body and pretending to catch his balance. Not much to be proud of, maybe. But he couldn't let her face this thing first. Not and salvage any sort of pride.

He gripped the edge of the boulder with his free hand and inched his head around.

After several seconds and a good rough poke in his ribs from Beth, Mark finally remembered to breathe.

"I don't think we can turn around and leave, Mr. Boun," he said, barely loud enough to hear. "Not any more."

Chapter 11

A TERRIFIED CORNER of Mark's mind kept shouting that he was looking into a volcano, a damn *volcano* in the middle of Boun County and *no one ever knew about it.*

But most of his mind knew that wasn't so, even without the aid and comfort of everything he'd ever learned in high school and college and grad school geology classes. He wasn't looking at any kind of natural occurrence.

Nothing that he'd ever heard of ran vertically along a wall of rock, for one thing.

The wall looked like typical limestone, except for the chalk-bright color instead of natural gray. Rippled and jagged enough to climb by hand if he was willing to touch it. Mark had often explored limestone caves as a kid, especially when he wasn't supposed to. Just another part of what got him into his career.

But none of those caves or the walls surrounding them had glowing red and orange lines and zigzags, like criss-crossing bolts of lightning had etched themselves onto the rocks.

Beth edged herself around between Mark's ribs and the

boulder he still held tight to. He was too stunned to stop her. He felt her body stiffen as she drew back, but she didn't look away.

She jumped hard enough to rattle Mark's teeth when another of those sharp cracks rang out.

Or maybe he jumped.

Either way, he saw a glowing fissure open in the wall in front of them.

"It *is* breaking open," Mark said, his voice high and shaky. "What the hell is trying to get out?"

Mr. Boun's voice was as just as trembly when he spoke.

"I never did hear tell of what it was or where it came from. No one here or there seems to know even after all these years. Might have been down in these mountains since they first rose up out of the land, or someone may have put it there. Only thing I can tell you is what it does, least when someone gets pushed down inside it."

"How'd you get inside it?" Beth said. She slipped her arm around Mark's waist and squeezed him hard enough to hurt. "You said it wasn't open before?"

"Is there any dark spot down there at the bottom? Like it got smudged with a bunch of charcoal?"

Mark leaned forward as far as he dared, which meant not letting go of the boulder or of Beth.

"There's no dark spot anywhere on it, sir. The whole thing is white as snow. I see kind of…might be a shadow down near the ground. That's where water's coming out now, but not very much."

"Water didn't run there, not as I recall," Mr. Boun said. "Not that high up. Such things alter over the years. But unless the whole cursed mountain has changed since my time on the earth came to an end, that shadow is the way in. The way I got *shoved* in, no matter how hard I fought or how loud I screamed. Nothing I did or any one else did could stop Reginald Hart when he set his mind to a thing."

"He set his mind to killing you?" Mark said. "To hiding you out here in some kind of demonic hole in the ground?"

"He set his mind to taking everything he could get from me or anyone else!" The anguished cry was even more disturbing for the way it echoed inside Mark's head.

Several other voices rose up, speaking all the different languages of people who'd come to work coal or timber and stayed on to raise families and live their lives. Gaelic and Welsh and German and Italian and Hungarian and Polish, and several others Mark couldn't recognize.

He did recognize that his harsh question had upset Mr. Boun enough for him to need calming down.

Beth knew it, too. But as in so many other things, she understood. She put her other arm around Mark and drew him back behind the two big boulders. Getting out of sight of the lightning-branded rock—and possible burying-alive site for Reginald Hart's enemies—let Mark untwist his nerves and muscles.

"I'm sorry, Mr. Boun," she said. "We're having trouble breathing here, and trouble figuring out what we can do to help."

"I'm very sorry, sir," Mark said. He turned to hug Beth full on, but he made sure he could still keep an eye on whatever the hell was going on upstream. "I didn't mean to upset you. Can I ask you if anything has changed over the last few weeks for you? Maybe since this…gate started to open?"

Mark's Papaw spoke up instead.

"I can tell you what you need to know on that one, water bug. Truth is I don't think Mr. Boun has been here all that long. Time don't pass the same once you cross over, but no one I spoke to since I last spoke with you has ever seen him before."

"I ain't never heard tell of him," Clina said. "We sure welcome him like we do anyone who finds their way here. But I think he came here from somewhere else. Maybe right there where you're standing."

Beth shivered and whispered close to Mark's ear.

"If he's been trapped here all this time, it truly is the gates of hell. Maybe he cracked it on his way out, chasing his damn teeth. And now the rest are breaking it open all the way."

"Can you ask him, Papaw?" Mark said quietly. "Gentle as you can? Ask if he moved from one place to another not very long ago."

After a few more seconds, Mark heard his Papaw's beloved raspy voice through all the background murmurs. He caught Mr. Boun's voice answering, but he couldn't catch the meaning. Only that those words had come out with a great deal of effort and pain.

"He's gone to crying," Clina said. "Folks sometimes do when they understand where we all are. Whatever happened to them that sent them here. But he don't sound sad or angry like so many do. I think Mr. Boun might be spilling over with happy tears."

"I'd say that's about right," Mark's Papaw said. "He told me he did just get here, after a long, dark time of not knowing where he was."

Mark startled so hard at the next crack of the stone that he drew in breath through his mouth, and regretted it terribly when the choking feeling was back in his throat and chest. If anything, the clammy, toxic air was getting worse.

Or else the filter on his respirator was about to fail.

"I'm afraid to ask this," he said. "And more afraid not to. Does Mr. Boun or any of you know if there are others? Still trapped here? Sounded like our dear Reginald Hart had more than one enemy he might have tucked away up here."

More muttered conversation, with Mr. Boun's tearful replies too low to hear.

"What are we going to do?" Mark said, drawing back enough to look into Beth's eyes.

"Fix it, if we can. Assuming these respirators hold out long enough."

Chapter 12

MARK WAS CAREFULLY DRAWING breath to admit he'd just been fretting about their respirators failing much too soon when Clina spoke.

"I'm sorry to say you're probably right about another lost soul. Mr. Boun said he'd been wandering around since he got here, looking for the ones he was caught with. Some met their end right there. Some Reginald Hart brought away from where they was properly laid to rest."

Mark closed his eyes, seeing water report data instead of maps this time.

"The other stuff in the water," Beth said. "Arsenic, right?"

"If he moved bodies here for some sick, twisted reason, that would explain it and the formaldehyde, too."

Mark peeked out around the boulders again, staring long and hard at the rock wall. Some parts he was sure were glowing earlier had faded to that unnatural white. The cracks were still there, but the red and orange color had gone.

"I think what we're hearing is the rock cracking," he said to Beth when she stepped around beside him. "You may be right about Mr. Boun doing that on his way out. See how the glow is fading? The cause may not be natural, but the heat from such a quick change might be. We can't get close enough to touch it with these little waterproof gloves either way."

She shook her head, wrinkling her nose under the respirator. Mark knew she'd hit upon a serious problem wondering if the small devices would last much longer. Besides the slowly clenching sensation in his airways, he was sure he smelled the rotten air more than he had a few minutes ago.

"Not between that and the rancid smell," she said. "Do you have something that could get closer? Equipment of some kind? Or bigger breathing gear?"

"Both," he said, nodding. "Back at the field office in Hartstown."

Besides spending all the time with Beth that he could manage, Mark had been slowly clearing out and restocking the tiny field office. Replacing dusty and outdated equipment with whatever he could gather from Richmond or the head-quarters over in Big Stone Gap. The supplies helped with the other expeditions out to old house pits and small, unper-mitted mines.

He hadn't expected to need them for another bizarre situation like this so soon.

He scowled. "This is my hometown, same place my family has lived for generations. But I don't know if I can stand to call it Hartstown anymore after this."

Beth returned his scowl when the tightness in his throat broke though into a series of harsh, painful coughs.

"Okay, that's enough," she said. "What do we need to do so we can get you out of here? Clina, the awful air is getting to both of us. I know Mr. Boun is upset, but can he give us any ideas?"

"He still wants you to get away from there," Clina said.

"Reckon I do too. You still got them teeth that washed up in the creek?"

Mark started to turn and let Beth dig them out of his pack, then dropped it off one shoulder and swung it around so he could get them himself. If the dreadful things were infected with whatever dwelled around Scatterland Creek, he'd rather she wasn't exposed to them.

Not that he was thrilled to touch them himself.

"Should we leave them here?" Mark said, holding the edges of the plastic bag with his fingertips.

"Mr. Boun keeps saying get the others, get the others," his Papaw said. "Over and over again. The ones trying to follow him out of that place. I keep telling him you said you can't get the other bodies right now, but I think he might mean those teeth. Does that make any sense to you, Mark? Beth? Can you see more?"

Mark stepped forward, the closest he'd dared to get to the vertical rock wall. To what he now believed was Reginald Hart's killing grounds.

A few more clumps of yellowed white stood out along the stream bed.

And his chest knotted up a little bit more.

"There are some here," he said. "Some back the way we came in." He hesitated, not wanting to upset anyone. But not speaking up and getting himself into real trouble would surely upset them more. He settled for a general warning that he hoped would be enough.

"We can get those," he said, "but then we probably need to get going. I'm worried about the filters in these respirators. We're both smelling it stronger, right?"

That earned him the angry glare from Beth and sharp, scolding words from his Papaw, Clina, and several other people in on the conversation.

"How long are they supposed to last?" Beth said,

brushing her fingertips along the blue circles at the bottom of her mask.

"They were fresh when we put them on. I replace them pretty much any time we use them, remember? Should have handled the air in a cave or an old mine for a lot longer than this. I never felt the air in any of those places gunk up against my skin like this, have you?"

Beth shook her head, but she couldn't hide the way she wrinkled her nose when she breathed again.

"Let's just get out of here," she said. "We know enough to come back later with better equipment."

Mark had no idea where it came from or when it would surface, but his stubborn streak—almost as big and powerful and deep as Beth's—reared up and demanded his attention. Maybe it responded to one of his own premonitions or dreams or visions, like his Papaw used to get.

"No, listen to me," he said. "If this place is getting worse as fast as it seems to be, we need to do whatever we can now. Maybe get a closer look at the entrance if there is one. If we just leave, this stink and everything that goes with it will make it even harder to come back. Right?"

Beth answered fast enough to prove she'd been thinking the same thing.

"We'll do that, but *I'm* getting the teeth. I don't like it, but one of us probably should see what the cave or whatever it is looks like. But don't you dare get too close, Mark!"

He shook his head, trying not to laugh at how badly he didn't want to get even one step closer. Laughing would draw too much of the sludgy air into his nose and mouth.

He dug out two pairs of elbow-length blue waterproof gloves and several of the clear plastic bags for the teeth. He slipped one pair of the gloves into his pocket, then handed everything else to Beth.

"Wish I'd brought an old digital camera I didn't mind

ruining instead of my phone," he said. "Don't touch the water any more than you have to."

She stared into his eyes for several seconds, long enough that he was sure she could tell how hard he was fighting to keep his breaths shallow.

"Don't *you* touch anything to do with that cave."

They walked toward the mouth of hell together.

Chapter 13

By the time Mark left Beth kneeling beside the creek, gloves on and plastic bag in hand, his eyes were watering from more than the stink. Sweat covered his face, turning the noxious air into what felt like a layer of glue.

The aroma of rotting fish joined the horror show inside his nose.

Another of those sharp cracks rang out, and this time he was close enough to see a streak along several feet of the rock wall split and glow red. Mark dragged his eyes away to concentrate on his footing. The creek was only a couple of inches deep, but ending up face first in such foul water was the stuff of his lifelong nightmares.

He could see from the closer angle that the waterway was new, cut through the mud and scattered bits of weeds left behind from last summer. Every single bit was faded to that shocking white, but Mark still recognized the sharper edges of a new rut.

"You okay, Beth?" he called over his shoulder. He missed being able to hear his Papaw terribly in that moment.

"Good as I can be. Just about got them all. You about finished?"

Mark stepped as close to the rock wall as he dared, close enough to feel the lingering head from the last few violent fractures.

Close enough that what little air he drew into his nose and lungs felt like molasses.

"Getting photos now," he said, fighting a horrible urge to start coughing.

The entrance didn't go straight down into the earth like he'd expected. Another split in the bright white rock—this one weathered and old instead of the sharp edges of the new breaks—opened straight back and shallow.

He snapped several pictures, then knelt on the muddy white ground to try to see farther inside. The opening was wider than his body, but it got narrow fast enough that he couldn't see the end of it. If anything, it sloped up a little bit. After a bunch more photos, Mark braced his hands on his knees to push himself up.

But he was tired enough that he just wanted to settle down right there.

Not for long, mind you.

Maybe rest for a little while, get his wind back, even through the reeking air.

If he was still, he wouldn't have to breathe all that hard anyway.

Only for a little while…

When Beth grabbed his arm, he realized he was on his feet but bent over, hands still on his knees, staring straight down into the new creek bed.

"Mark! Don't you *dare* pass out on me. I can't carry you all the way back down to the car!"

Clina, his Papaw, and everyone else erupted inside his head again, and he didn't have to know the languages to understand the meaning. He figured he deserved any amount of scolding, and it might just wake him up.

He let Beth pull him to a standing position, hoping he didn't grip her hand and arm too tight when the world faded and tilted.

"I won't pass out," he said. His voice sounded tinny, like it passed through a cheap speaker. "Not feeling great, though. Time to go."

They turned to head downstream, her arm around his waist and his around her shoulder, and everything slowly turned too bright. The white of the mud and rocks and plants seemed to glow, like they were backlit.

He realized his lungs didn't only feel tight now. They were burning, as if he'd just run a couple of miles way too fast.

"Still with me?" Beth said. "What's three plus eight?"

"Eleven. Not quite that bad yet. Listen, soon as you get signal, or I do, call Art. Just in case you need help dragging my carcass out of here."

"Hilarious. Keep that up and I'll leave you here on purpose."

"Not just for that," Mark said. "See if he can get in touch with the woman who sold him the land. The one who got it clear cut and made sure it was done wrong." He gritted his teeth against a greasy wave of nausea. "She in…inherited it, so she might…might know more."

When they got to the last spot where the air was clear on the way up, they paused long enough for Beth to lift the edge of her mask. She groaned and settled it back into place.

"Not as bad as up there, but not clear. You're pouring sweat all the way through your clothes, Mark. Still hanging in?"

"Ugh, you're right." He tried to draw away from her, but she held tight. "I'm sorry."

"Let's get you back and we'll worry about that later. Neither one of us is especially clean after being in that air anyway."

The brightness got worse, and now Mark felt like he was too tall. His feet took forever to find the ground, longer with each step. Harsh ringing in his ears disconnected him from his feet even more, since he couldn't hear the sound of his own steps anymore.

Worse of all, the floaty feeling in his head brought the nausea back full force.

Beth's voice reached him down a long, twisting tunnel.

"…right here, Art, but he's about to fall over and take me with him. …could definitely say it's worse. …meet us out here at…"

Mark lost his struggle not to cough then, doubling over hacking and choking. He knew he was going to overload the portable unit with carbon dioxide out of his own body and end up breathing his own used up air, but he couldn't stop.

Beth braced herself in front of him and helped ease him to his knees.

He tried to stop her from lifting the mask from his sweaty face.

"No, sweetie, the air's okay. You're doing yourself more harm than good. Breathe now, Mark. Come on. Get yourself calmed down and I'll get you some water."

The coughing went on and on until he saw bright spots and was sure he had to be bringing up blood. He'd ended up with pneumonia once after a horrible bout with the flu when he was in his twenties. He'd coughed up blood then, but he didn't remember choking quite this much.

He didn't even realize Beth had left until she came back. He jerked back from a cool circle of metal against his lips.

"Here, drink. Come on now, get some of this down."

Mark forced his eyes open and was startled to see normal

brown mud that was way too close to his face. A few clumps of green weeds hung on nearby, and the metal water bottle Beth held up to his mouth was bright red. Light-headed and loopy as he was still feeling, seeing any color besides the dead white around that cave made him feel a hundred percent better.

But nothing matched his relief at turning his head enough to see Beth's blue eyes.

He drank, coughed again, then managed to drink until the bottle was empty.

"Okay, good." Beth knelt beside him, rubbing his back. "There's more in the car. Think you can walk a little more now?"

He spoke through a throat that felt (and sounded) full of glass.

"You got all of them? The teeth?"

Beth shook her head, but Mark caught her amused, annoyed expression.

"That really is what you're worried about, isn't it? Never mind you coughing yourself half to death. Yes Mark. I got them. Listen, Mr. Boun's quiet now."

He sat back on his heels, wishing he had more water but relieved he could breathe again. He heard the low mutter of voices, but no one was crying or yelling.

"That boy's always been like that, Beth," Mark's Papaw said. "Stubborn as the rising and setting sun. I always was thankful he's so dang tough to go with it."

Mark wiped the back of his hand across his mouth, saw no blood, and smiled up at Beth. She helped him get to his feet again, and he was so thankful to be able to stand on his own that he almost started crying right there.

"Tough and hard-headed pretty much have to go together for a person to survive for long," he said. "At least we managed to grab something. I forgot to get samples of that white moss, but I'll just have to wait on that. Did I hear you talking to Art?"

She nodded, and Mark felt a pang of guilt to go with his finally clearing head when he took a good look at her. Her curly brown hair was flat and stiff with sweat, her face pale and cheeks flushed. He'd taken more of a toll on her than he ever meant to.

"Damn right you'll wait on getting that moss or anything else," she said. "Art will get here fast as he can. He's probably already down there waiting. I don't think it's even half a mile walk."

Mark caught her hand and pulled her tight against him, hoping he didn't stink quite as bad as the air around the bizarre cave.

"I'm sorry, Beth. You were absolutely right to insist on us working together out here. Turns out I'm the one who needed the assist after all. I didn't mean for you to have to drag me away from the portal to the underworld or whatever that damn thing is."

She laughed under her breath.

"You forget I leaned on your back all the way down the mountain in November, and we hardly knew each other then. I wouldn't mind if things were a hell of a lot less dramatic on a daily basis, but I figure if we can help each other out once in a while, we'll do okay."

Chapter 14

Neither Art nor Beth would confirm or deny that the hot tea, honey, horehound, and cayenne pepper mixture was spiked with anything stronger. Mark's nose—and the near-instant relief in his throat—left him strongly suspicious. As did a smoky flavor an awful lot like what his Papaw mixed up when he was sick in the middle of the night years ago.

He didn't care one way or the other, not with the way the stuff worked. He just hoped they'd share the recipe with him someday.

After the third day of hot, scrubbing showers and long, bubbly baths, he and Beth finally agreed they felt and smelled normal again. Janie finally stopped wrinkling her sensitive hound dog nose at both of them around that same time.

Beth managed to get her sorely overworked shoulder loosened up not long after.

That also happened to be how long it took for Art to convince Melanie Ruddin to take his calls, and to agree to fly in from Denver. Mark was sure Art's tales of finding a collection of sinister teeth did it much more than his own bad reaction to the logging site.

Art managed to work similar magic with Mr. Powell, Mark's supervisor back in Richmond. He told Mark to consider this prolonged assignment a trial run. A perfect way to see how they both managed with him operating from several hours away.

Whatever the reason—or the number of favors being called in on his behalf—Mark was grateful beyond reason for the time. Time to recover, time with Beth, and time to figure out what on earth they'd walked into the middle of.

Dealing with the most noxious of air and water was part of Mark's line of work, and his and Beth's quick visit had left him nearly flat on his back. Much as they hated to, they agreed to wait on getting anyone else up there to try to extract any remains.

Once they understood more, if anyone could help with Scatterland Creek, with problems natural or unnatural, they'd take every bit of that help.

Because something about that place was decidedly *un*natural. Melanie and whatever she knew could only help, certainly combined with everything Beth and Art had unearthed at the town hall and the courthouse.

The deeper the two of them dug, the more they turned up to confirm Mr. Boun's tales about Reginald Hart. They'd taken to discreetly sneaking all the faded or flood-damaged letters, police and coroners reports, and bank receipts out and squirreling them away at Art's office, sprawled out across his dining-room-sized oak work table or tucked away inside his own safe.

A combination of air purification machines, open windows, and frequent breaks combated the worst of the rancid, sulfurous stink the collected materials managed to generate. Mark was equal parts embarrassed and disgusted to find himself affected more by the smell than either Art or Beth. And equally unable to do anything about it but volunteer to run errands and fetch lunch for the entire office staff.

By the time Melanie Ruddin was scheduled to arrive six days after their Scatterland misadventure, everything was organized, neatly boxed up, and ready for inspection.

Mark didn't know quite who he expected when they met Melanie at Art's office that morning. But she surprised him from the second she walked in.

Melanie was tiny and delicate, with pale skin, light brown eyes, and red hair cut short enough to emphasize the almost elfin quality of her features. She stood barely as tall as Mark's chest. Beth towered over her, too, and made Melanie look more like a porcelain doll than a grown woman older than either of them.

Melanie's cheery golden jacket and pants put an image of her perched on top of a spring daffodil into Mark's head for some crazy reason, one he tried unsuccessfully to banish.

Despite her appearance, she carried a huge black bag that would have been too big for an airline carry-on with no apparent effort. After she thumped it onto the massive, polished surface of Art's work table, she proceeded to shake everyone's hands with a firm, cool grip.

Her voice struck Mark exactly the same way. Firm and cool.

"Strange to be meeting you for the first time, Mr. Steffens. Certainly after our many conversations this week. I'm Melanie."

Obviously charmed, Art grinned and ducked his head.

"Call me Art, please. I insist. We sure do appreciate you coming all this way to try to help us out."

"I only hope I *can* help," Melanie said after speaking to Beth and Mark in turn. She sank down into a chair beside her bag with a deep sigh. "I'm afraid my actions caused a lot of the trouble you've been going through. Mine and my oh-so-lovely quadruple-great-grandfather."

"You mean Reginald Hart?" Beth said, joining Mark on the other side of the table.

"That's him," Melanie said. "I ended up with the land and the house by attrition, I think. No one else wanted it, and by the time my great-auntie passed on, I was the only one she was still in touch with. To tell you the truth, there weren't that many of us. Only a handful of cousins of various flavors among his descendants. Odd, don't you think, after all this time?"

"It's unusual for sure," Mark said. "The last Hersch reunion I got dragged to when I was a teenager probably had a couple hundred people there. Do you know what happened to the house?"

Melanie took a deep breath before she stood and closed the door. Back at the table, she closed her eyes for a few seconds before she folded her hands on the surface and looked at Art.

"I burned it to the ground. I've never said that out loud, not to anyone. Of course since I haven't set foot in Bounty-field since that day, I'm not sure who I would have told in the first place."

Art opened his mouth, then closed it hard enough his teeth clicked.

"That's probably the last thing I expected to hear you say," he finally said. He leaned back in his chair, brushing his fuzz of steel gray hair smooth against his scalp. "About the fire, not calling the place Bountyfield. What little we've turned up has me calling it that instead of Hartstown. I don't suppose you're technically my client at this moment, but I'll treat this the same as if you were, okay? I have to ask why you resorted to arson."

"I figured you would," Melanie said. "First of all, I made

several sizable donations to the volunteer fire department in my auntie's name for about a year before I did it. All out of money that passed down from dear old Quad Great himself. That helped me a little with the guilt."

She worked a tiny silver combination lock Mark hadn't noticed, then flipped the bag open flat like an oversized briefcase.

"I burned it because of these. Reginald Hart's diaries and correspondences. All tucked away and safe in hidden compartments all over that damn house. I never much liked what I heard about him when I was a kid, but reading a few of these things sent me scrambling to research how to cause an electrical fire in an old house without getting caught."

Mark tried to keep his features calm, but he pushed back in his chair, muscles tense along his arms and legs and back with the effort.

The folded bundles and stacks and rolls of yellowing paper smelled exactly like Scatterland Creek. More like the strange cave at the head of it, actually.

Beth's hand on his quivering thigh made him jump, but he managed to let out the breath he'd been holding. He still didn't want to touch anything in that bag, though.

"Did this have anything to do with what happened out at the land?" he said, moving his chair back and watching Beth and Art pick through the documents. "Before you sold it to Art, I mean."

Melanie nodded once.

"It did. I'm more sorry about that than the house. That was easy enough to let burn out and bulldoze under, from what I hear. I shouldn't have made such a mess out on the land, especially when I didn't understand what would happen. No one could, I suppose, but I acted without thinking it through. I couldn't figure out a way to burn several mountains down, so I did the closest thing I could think of and hired the worst crew I could find. Art tells me the result hit you hardest, Mark. Are you feeling better?"

He blinked, not the least bit sure what to say now that everyone's attention turned to him. His Papaw whispered in his mind, even without Beth's touch.

"It's all gonna be just fine, water bug."

"I'm okay, doing better. The only trouble I'm still having is…well, the smell. All these papers are full of the same thing the water was."

"That was another reason I burned the place down," Melanie said. "Once I opened up all the hiding places for Quad Great's nightmares, the whole house reeked of it. I don't think anyone could have ever scrubbed it clean with all the bleach in the world."

Mark managed to smile despite his urge to get away from the stench.

"To be painfully honest, it might be for the best that all that timber was cut down and hauled away. I can't imagine anything that grew so close to that cave ever being clean or good, either."

Beth cleared her throat, in the slow, deliberate way Mark knew meant she had something to say. Something she didn't particularly *want* to say.

Chapter 15

"Do you think Mr. Hart honestly believed what he wrote here?" She tapped the leather-bound diary open in front of her. "That he was purifying the town, getting rid of evil people who would cause all their virtuous endeavors to fail?"

Melanie shook her head, then stared down at the table. That was the first time Mark noticed her not calmly looking into someone's eyes.

"I don't know what to believe there," she said quietly. "Once I realized he did such horrible things, I stopped wondering much about *why* he did them. If he truly believed he was engaging in some kind of purification ritual by murdering Mr. Boun and the others, and increasing the potency by dragging people he decided stood against him out of the graveyard and stashing them on his land, does that make what he did any less awful?"

Art rubbed the back of his neck and looked at Beth with his eyebrows raised, waiting for her to nod.

"We found a few records that made it sound like he was killing people," he said. "No one came right out and said it, of course, but several people seemed convinced. Someone was worried enough to misfile all of it, hide it away. Or maybe they were told to so Mr. Hart wouldn't destroy it. Did you find solid proof in that house?"

Melanie looked at Art and held out her hands, palms up.

"I don't know how we could truly prove it all these years later. Do you? All I know is he wrote about it in great detail, then went to the trouble of hiding it all away. Then there's the smell."

"Part of that makes sense," Mark said, "with the way that cave smelled. If he spent a whole lot of time out there, maybe it would linger. But I've never run across anything that *feels* like that. Like walking through a wall of rancid glue."

He turned to Beth then, wondering how much he should say about Clina and his Papaw and everyone else with Art and Melanie able to hear every word. Thankfully, Beth seemed to understand. She grabbed his hand under the table.

"…heard tell of cold spots," Clina was saying. "Places you walk through and it feels like you got yanked into the dead of winter. Nothing that feels like what you say, thick on your skin."

"I ran across a place or two like that," Mark's Papaw said, his words slow and soft. "Kind of place you felt like you had to run through fast as you could, but the bad parts came with you. Had to scrub off in the bathtub for a good long time to get rid of that."

Mark held his hand over his mouth, hoping it looked like he was trying to avoid the stink growing in the room.

"Where was that, Papaw?" he whispered, as quietly as he could.

"Couple of times I went hunting with my brothers, once over near Lightning Gap. Then out toward Estonoa, and Holly Creek. Never did think much of it, to tell you the truth. Not 'till all this come up."

He glanced at Beth, then turned to get a good look at

her. She had one corner of her mouth turned up, and a sparkle in her eyes that seemed entirely out of place with the macabre conversation.

She let go of his hand and jumped up fast enough to send her chair scooting back. She moved one of the white boxes stacked against the wall and dug into the one underneath.

"We might have the proof, Melanie," she said. "You were talking about Reginald Hart not having many descendants. What about Zachary Boun? How many does he have? Anyone know?"

A warm spark of excitement started up in Mark's belly. Whether they found any quad-great Bouns or not, Beth's fantastic, fascinating mind might have just made the leap they all needed.

"Family lore always was that we're descendants of his," Art said, watching Beth with his head tilted to the side. "You never know with stories like that with folks who like to run their mouths, but I'd be happy to volunteer a little spit to find out. Think you might scrape enough DNA out of those teeth to make it worthwhile?"

Beth walked back over and dropped the two plastic bags of teeth onto the table.

"It's worth a try, don't you think?" she said, leaning forward with her hands flat on the table. "From what you have here, Melanie, and what we found, I'd bet we'll find bones buried down in that stinking cave, too. Maybe the skulls these came out of, or that they got knocked out of."

"They have a great genetics department at Virginia Tech," Mark said, smiling. "If they can't help us out, they'd know who could. We'll need much tougher respirators and digging equipment, but I'd say you're right about the bones. Wouldn't it be something to prove Mr. Boun didn't simply disappear? Maybe get his bones and everyone else's properly buried, just like our miner's?"

Melanie frowned, and Mark realized she probably had no idea what he was talking about.

"We'll explain it all later," Beth said. She shifted her hands into fists against the table, then sat beside Mark again. "This may give us a way to prove what happened over a hundred years ago. But did you find anything in his house that might explain why the rocks, the mud, even all the plants out there are all dead white?"

Melanie's eyes widened, then the color drained from her already pale skin. She turned to Art and opened her mouth twice before any words escaped.

"You didn't tell me about that, Art. I don't know if I would have stayed away or gotten here sooner if you had." She shook her head, held one hand against her throat, and took a deep breath.

"I can't believe I'm about to say this out loud," she said. "My ancestor Reginald Hart got pretty heavily into…occult beliefs and activity. Partly because of a trip to London he took a few years after the end of the Civil War. He met up with a few practitioners there. And, well, he brought it back here and made it his own. As far as I can tell, with literal blood sacrifices."

"That's all in these diaries?" Beth said. She sat back from the one open on the table as if she was too afraid to touch it. "What he did and why he did it?"

"I'm afraid so, Beth. I wouldn't recommend reading it if you ever want to sleep at night without horrible dreams. I still have nightmares."

"We may not have much choice," Mark said, looking at Beth, then Art. Both were pale and shaken. "If we're going to undo whatever he did. Make it stop somehow. Like you said, we can't burn down the mountains. That might only make the problem worse if we could."

Melanie scowled and shook her head, the expression odd on her delicate features.

"You're not telling me you believe he actually was onto something with all his rites and rituals? What he wrote… Murdering people is one thing, and more than bad enough. If he actually did even half that other stuff, the only thing we know for sure is he was crazier than I thought."

Beth smiled at Mark and held his hand under the table again.

"We've both learned the hard way that sometimes we have to accept what's happening before we can solve it. I think Art knows more than he lets on, but Mark and I had a strange experience last year. One that keeps us from dismissing something like this without learning more."

Mark shrugged. "It may not be exactly the occult stuff that got written down that he was doing in the end. You may have been on the right track by saying he made it his own. Almost anyone who's spent much time here wouldn't deny there's all kinds of old magic that lingers in these mountains."

Melanie stared at him hard for a few seconds before she spoke.

"Much as I want to, and I really do want to, I can't disagree."

"Maybe it worked *because* he brought it here," Mark said. "Getting back to what we can prove with science, I suspect that cave is a natural sulfur spring now that something changed the water flow. Wouldn't be surprised if there was methane venting, too, from how hard it hit me. Who knows how that interacted with what he was doing?"

"One of the things we talk about all the time in the law is intent," Art said, steepling his fingers in front of his face. "Whether a person meant to do harm or not. Or what they were honestly trying to do. Mr. Hart is no different. He may have brought an intent, a determination, that changed everything he did."

Melanie pursed her lips, then sat back with a sigh.

"I imagined this meeting going about a hundred different ways on the flight and the drive out here. From wishful thinking about mistaken identity to me getting taken away in handcuffs as a firebug." She laughed under her breath. "Now I'm wondering if all four of us are about to get hauled away for even considering…what we're considering."

"Don't know why y'all don't just take her up there," Clina said through Beth's touch, and Mark once again hoped he hid his reflexive jump. "See how fast she squalls like a spooked cat and goes running back home."

Beth coughed, and Mark was sure she was trying to hide laughter.

"How about this," he said, squeezing her hand. "You're here for what, three days, Melanie? I have heavy-duty safety gear, enough for all of us. I can get equipment brought in to excavate the cave later on, if nothing else to investigate the arsenic and formaldehyde in the water."

No one disagreed and they were all still listening, so he went on.

"The three of us read what we can stomach this afternoon and tonight to get ready. See if your Quad Great left hints of how we might reverse what he did. You read through what Art and Beth dug up out of town records. We meet up here and compare notes. If that all works out the way I think it will, we all head out to Scatterland Creek together."

Chapter 16

THE MEETING the next morning was mercifully quick. Once everyone got past sharing what they'd learned, and what they hoped might work, no one felt much like talking. No one had felt much like breakfast, either.

Sunny and clear skies pointed out another problem to Mark, one he'd been thinking more about with every passing day. As far as he'd been able to tell from records and his own observations, Scatterland Creek's true headwaters were below Reginald Hart's murderous cave. The water now flowing out —along with the stink and maybe the horrible feeling to the air—seemed to be related to the rough winter just past and heavy spring rains.

So if his theory was true, and their luck held, the water coming out of the cave should be dwindling by now. Maybe making the atmosphere less toxic.

If his theory was wrong, or if the fifty percent chance of rain tilted in the wrong direction, conditions around Art's land could be even worse.

As they all piled into Art's trusty old Jeep Cherokee, Mark decided to keep that worry to himself for now. If the much heavier-duty full-face respirators he had in the back didn't do the trick, they'd simply have to do this another time, or another way. Not one of them needed one more thing on their minds after their reading and study of the night before.

If Art and Melanie had passed as long and difficult a night as Mark and Beth had, they might be running on less than eight hours sleep between them.

Even Clina, Mark's Papaw, and Mr. Boun were silent. Beth had admitted when they shared coffee and picked bleary-eyed at breakfast that everyone in the next world had been with her most of the night, too. All their talking and fretting had strangely kept her company. Mark regretted not listening in himself.

He helped fit everyone's clear full-face masks, thinking how a quick lesson in how to clear and seal them would have seemed like overkill only a few days before. But the lingering traces of a cough had Mark showing them all how to cover the round black exhalation valve in front, then blow out to remove any traces of tainted air. Covering the thick purple filters on the sides while breathing in pulled masks tight.

After a couple of practice runs, he settled the masks loose around necks or clipped onto belts.

One more nervous check through his backpack full of the usual random supplies and a few extras, and he was out of reasons to delay heading up the muddy but still normal creek.

When they made it to the odd curve of rock in the creek bed he remembered as the end of breathable air on his and Beth's first walk up, Mark finally managed to speak.

"Anyone catching an unusual smell, good or bad?"

They stared at each other but avoided his eyes, reminding him of students doing their best to keep from getting called on in class.

"Don't worry, it's not a test. I'm just curious."

He pulled a compact black multi-gas detector out of his pocket, not much bigger than a smart phone but heavier. The edges were rubberized with knobs and contours for protection and better grip, and an old-fashioned gray LED display with black markings took up the bottom.

The most important part today was the orange and white lights along the top.

"This picks up methane, carbon monoxide, sulfur dioxide, and oxygen, and lets us know when they rise or fall to dangerous levels." He winced at the wide eyes and startled looks. "*If*, I mean. *If* they hit dangerous levels. I'll be honest, I'm more than a little upset with myself for not bringing it last week. I didn't expect what we ran into. But even if I had, our own senses work best for some things."

Beth nodded, finally meeting Mark's gaze.

"If even a quarter of what we all read is true," she said, "we're not looking for any kind of natural smell, anyway. Or not only that. Reginald Hart's cave might require human senses."

Art rubbed at his goatee, even more closely trimmed to prevent interference with the respirator.

"I don't smell anything yet. I didn't notice it the first time until I walked quite a bit higher."

"So it's retreating," Mark said. "The smell, it's not as strong here as when Beth and I walked out. At least for now. The colors are still normal, too."

Melanie squatted and examined the creek bed, all the ordinary stones and plants and water. Jeans and a dark green button up shirt instead of her cheery golden suit transformed her from businesswoman into a dedicated outdoorsy resident of Colorado.

Mark had an outdated but terribly effective jolt of little boy fear. He was sure they were going to walk up to the top of the trail, past the creek bed and the new waterway and all the way to the cave, and not a single odd thing would be there.

The air would smell normal, and the mud and rocks and plants would look normal, and Melanie and even Art would accuse him of making the whole thing up.

Having Beth by his side, with the same memories of the gluey, toxic air, helped with that irrational fear. But it didn't quite go away.

"You said things turn white?" Melanie said. "The closer you get to the cave?"

"The moss and small plants in the water at first," Beth said. "Then some small oak trees, the mud, and the limestone itself. The only color in there at the top was those damn teeth."

"And the rock wall after it split," Mark said, still trying to convince himself of what he'd seen. "It glowed orange and hot, because of the break, I think. We saw a couple of them fade."

Instead of rolling her eyes or maybe pulling out another childhood throwback and twirling her index finger beside her temple, Melanie nodded to herself as she stood.

"I'd say that fits with what we all read last night. You now all know how my lovely Quad Great started out wishing for class purity, from what he picked up in London. Then he was on to racial purity, of course, thanks to all the Civil War excitement, even in this end of Virginia."

"He really did make it his own," Art said. "Once he focused on the purity of people who shared his glorious vision for Boun County."

"People who agreed that to him alone should go all the glory," Beth said. She closed her eyes and shook her head. "I'm sorry, Melanie. That was mean. I think what I read and not getting enough sleep have eroded my manners."

Melanie snorted and put her hands on her hips.

"Do you have any idea how many sleepless nights that asshole has caused me, from a hundred years in his grave? Even before I broke into his secret stash and found out who he really was? I wouldn't expect *anyone* sane to mind their manners when it comes to Reginald Hart."

"Fair enough," Beth said, smiling at Melanie and grabbing Mark's hand. "Let's go see what we've gotten ourselves into."

Clina's sharp laughter blended nicely with the raspy guffaws from Mark's grandfather.

"Found yourselves a good'un there," Clina said. "Might be able to work this thing out yet."

The water continued at lower levels, the air clear, and the ground normal until Mark spotted the bleached out moss in the same spot as before.

"I see why that got your attention," Melanie said.

This time Mark knelt beside her, blue waterproof gloves on and sample bag in hand.

"You're taking it?" Melanie said. "What for?"

"Well, I meant to when we were here before." Mark carefully pulled a solid mat of the moss up, making sure to get the whole thing. He scooped a few handfuls of water into the bag to try to keep it fresh. "But I wasn't in any shape to remember on the way back out. I'll send this to Richmond and get the moss and the water analyzed. No matter what we figure out today, I want to know more about what happened here."

"And that," Art said, beaming, "is why I insisted on Mark Hersch and no one else for this situation. Hey, didn't you two say the smell started before the white plants did?"

Mark looked into Beth's wide blue eyes. She nodded.

"It did, but I just smell mud," she said. "Some kind of chemical undertone, but nothing like before."

"Yeah, same here," Mark said. "I think that's gas or oil from the lumber crew. This thing is retreating. I wondered if it might with a few days of no rainfall."

Melanie shivered, rubbing her upper arms.

"Retreating? Or retracting? Drawing itself up, getting concentrated?"

Beth turned and stared up the creek, then back toward Art's Jeep and escape back into the normal world.

"That's exactly what one of those diary entries said. He decided to add the blood sacrifice, and later the bodies he dug up, to *concentrate* his efforts. That's why he crushed their skulls, too, knocked their teeth out. To make the whole spell or construct or whatever he called it stronger."

Mark glanced at the sky, making note of the grayish cloud cover building up to the west.

Not threatening, not yet. But not something they could ignore.

"If the tough winter and spring rain caused this to break open," he said, "more rain will only make it worse. If it is concentrated and stronger, we might not be able to stop it."

The strange light in Melanie's eyes made him more uncomfortable than the idea of getting caught near Hart's cave during a downpour.

"I'm ready," she said. "This whole thing has haunted me long enough."

Chapter 17

THE WHITE DISCOLORATION continued to spread along the creek, the plants, and the ground like it had before, but they only caught drifts of the sulfur stink on the shifting winds. It didn't kick into full strength until Mark caught sight of the ghostly white oaks tucked in close to the big boulders.

Art wrinkled his nose and turned aside, scrambling for the mask Mark had clipped onto his belt back at the road.

"That is worse," he said, his voice choked and rough. "You and Beth walked through *this?*"

"Not the whole time," Beth said. She cleared and sealed her full-face mask as if she'd done it a thousand times. "Feel that? The way the air is too thick?"

"We should have hazmat suits for this," Melanie said. "Or a drone or something like it."

Mark smiled, still distracted by what he was now sure was excitement in Melanie's face and voice.

"The budget for this project didn't quite cover drones or robotic assistance. I haven't heard any of those cracks, either. Look at the creek bed."

The white mud and rocks were still there, but the trickling water was gone, leaving the sharp edges of the new path it had carved on its way out.

"The cave is just past those boulders," Beth said. She watched Melanie, too. "If the rock isn't breaking right now, we won't have to worry about the heat. But the air was bad enough over there to almost take Mark out."

Mark heard the words Beth didn't say, and he hoped Melanie did, too.

The poisonous sludge had done a vicious number on a man who was probably close to twice Melanie's weight, and who had close to twenty years experience dealing with impaired air and water.

Melanie adjusted her mask and stepped forward.

"What was the other thing old Quad Great said? The blood and bodies anchored what he was doing. Gave it a focus. I wonder what would happen if those anchors were gone?"

And she walked around the boulders and out of sight.

Mark tried his trick of scooting around to get in front of Beth, but she was on to him, and too fast.

He and Art rounded the corner just in time to see Melanie's well-worn hiking boots disappear into the cave at the bottom of the solid white wall.

Chapter 18

BETH DARTED FORWARD and crouched on the dead white
ground.

"Melanie! None of us can reach you in there!"

Mark landed hard on his knees beside her, heart
pounding in his throat.

He drew in a breath before he raised his mask long
enough to shout.

"The air may be even worse in there! Watch out!"

Art stood close enough behind them to touch.

"Can you see her? Or hear anything?"

"Not a damn thing," Mark said. He scooted back enough
to get flat down on his belly.

"Don't make this worse, Mark," Beth said, grabbing his
belt. "You didn't do so well with that gas before."

He raised up enough to look at her. "I can't smell it yet,
can you? These filters are stronger. I'm just going to try to see
where she is."

He pushed himself forward through mud as slimy and
thick as the air, glancing at the white rock over his head.
None of the glowing orange streaks were there today.

But they had no way to know when that might start up again.

Or if the cracks had made the cave itself unstable.

"Melanie," he called. "Yell back if you can hear me."

He turned his head to the side, held his breath, and listened.

Silence.

Not even the noise of someone crawling through the passage.

Mark pushed himself forward, head inside the cave, shoulders pressing uncomfortably against the walls.

The air compressed around him even more, like a tunnel of rancid flesh.

Beth tightened her grip on his belt and tugged.

"Mark, at least test the air before you go one more inch."

He twisted his arm back enough to grab the multi-gas detector and held it in front of his face.

"Sulfur dioxide, methane," he said. "High, not lethal. Oxygen lower than I'd like, but okay for a few minutes. I can't *go* one more inch, anyway."

A loud scrape and a grunt sounded in front of him.

"Melanie, if you can hear me, the air isn't safe in there. We can bring equipment back and excavate the whole thing."

Her voice sounded muffled and more distant than he liked when she finally answered.

"You just said it was okay for a few minutes. Walls pure yellow in here, only white along the bottom where it's muddy. Bones and awful drawings and lines everywhere. Gonna use the mud to smudge those out."

The sound Mark had been dreading in the back of his mind rumbled through the rock around him.

"Beth, Art, was that thunder?"

Beth eased her grip but she didn't let go.

"It was. Art says the clouds are starting to pile up to the west."

"Behind this cave, you mean," Mark said. The walls somehow felt even tighter. "Where the floodwater must have come from. Melanie? Sounds like it's going to rain. We have to come back and do this later."

A sharp, painfully loud crack rang out.

"Please tell me that was lightning," Mark said.

"I don't think so," Beth said. "I can't see anything, but it sounded more like how the rock was breaking."

Mark realized the white rock in front of him had taken on an orange tinge, and the cave felt warmer. He shrank down against the bottom of the passage and managed to look up.

"It was the rock breaking," he said. "Right over my head." He raised his voice. "This cave might be unstable, Melanie. We have to get out, *now*."

Beth and Art's words were drowned out by Mark's grandfather inside his head.

"You best *listen* to me, Andrew Mark Hersch! You get yourself clear of there, and you do it right this second!"

Another sharp crack, loud enough to leave Mark's ears ringing, was more than enough to convince him.

When he started backing out, Beth put both hands on his belt and dragged him free. She squeezed him hard with her strong left arm, not noticing or not caring about the disgusting white mud all over him.

Art squatted in front of the cave in the flat spot Mark left.

"Whatever you're doing seems to be making things worse," he yelled. "If the roof slips, we won't be able to get you out of there!"

A few more scraping noises, and a mutter that Mark was sure started out as "shit."

"I'm getting out now," Melanie said. "Getting hot in here, and wet. Can't stand the stink any more. Someone grab my hands?"

Mark drew back from Beth, fighting the urge to wipe the muck off her her shirt and face. He surely looked worse. Before he could stretch out on the ground again, Art beat him to it with Beth by his side.

Thunder rumbled again, much closer.

"Can you see her?" Mark said, kneeling behind Beth.

"I don't… Yes! Grab my hand!"

Two more cracks, and two jagged orange lines opened up right above the cave entrance. The heat felt like it would bake the mud dry on Mark's skin and clothes.

Shocking cold around his knees let him know he'd landed right in the new creek bed.

And that the fouled water was flowing again.

His next breath carried the reek of the portal to the underworld.

Art stretched forward at the same time Beth did.

"Got it," Art said. He shifted and worked his hand out, holding something long and thin and yellowish. "Grab it, Mark. So I can get her other hand."

The thing was a human femur.

"What the *hell* would I want with this?" Mark tossed it on the ground behind him and wiped his hands on his muddy shirt.

Before anyone could answer, thunder almost drowned out a crack loud enough to echo against the treeless hills around them.

Now Mark could see much farther into the cave, enough to see Art and Beth holding Melanie's forearms. The flat opening had transformed into an upside down V.

"Hang on!" Beth shouted. "We're going to pull!"

Mark followed her example, grabbed both Beth's and Art's belts, and did just that.

He fell backward with a splash; the foul, stinking water and mud covering his backside as well as his front.

Beth and Art sprawled back onto Mark's legs, with Melanie face down in between the two of them.

"Melanie?" Beth said, pushing Melanie's shoulder. "Come on, are you okay?"

No one moved for several painfully tense seconds.

Melanie's back slowly rose and fell, and she lifted her head.

Mark realized just then that she was covered in yellow gunk with splotches of white, all the way up the front of her mask.

"I think…got it all. Those drawings and lines. Covered them up. The bones. Rotted clothing. Couldn't get… Not all of them." She curled up then, caught up in a coughing fit every bit as awful as Mark's had been on the first encounter with the cave.

A huge crash overhead had all four of them scrambling to their feet, with a few rather painful jabs to Mark's anatomy.

"Thunder," he said, trying to catch his breath. "There's the rain. We'd better get out of here."

"How long were these respirators supposed to work?" Art said. The clear plastic of his mask was streaked with white and yellow mud, but his grimace was plain to see.

"Should have been several more hours," Mark said. "The same thing happened up here before. We can't stay."

Just then the gas detector in his pocket let out a harsh, buzzing alarm.

That somehow worked better than his words had to get everyone moving.

They headed back downstream, Beth and Mark supporting Melanie, with water rising under their feet and the air getting worse by the second. They'd just rounded the boulders and the oak trees when Melanie dug in her heels. She managed to speak through more throat-wrenching coughs.

"The bone. Did…did someone get it?"

Mark blinked, finally remembering throwing it behind him.

"I'm sorry, I didn't know you wanted to keep it."

Art dashed back and returned in record time just as huge raindrops started to fall.

"Got it. Zachary Boun, I presume?"

Even through the dirty mask, Mark saw her elfin smile.

"Part of him, I hope. It was right in the middle of everything."

Beth nodded, meeting Mark's gaze.

"Then let's get at least that much of him out of here," she said. "Get him laid to rest. Sometimes that can make all the difference in the world."

Chapter 19

July 4th dawned sunny and warm, and Mark was more grateful for the cool breeze that played along the mountains and valleys than he wanted to admit. Boun County could get hot and humid, but nothing like the sodden, heavy summers in Richmond.

Summers he'd soon be leaving behind.

The crowd gathering around the town square was bigger than he ever remembered from visits when he was a kid. The scent of popcorn and hotdogs had his stomach growling in anticipation exactly the same way it had back then. The pale gray steps leading up the blocky gray courthouse were packed full except for the very top, with streets closed all around to handle the overflow out of the grassy park in the middle.

Everyone milled around and chatted and buzzed with excitement, creating a dull roar that managed to drown out the train passing only a few blocks away. People had shown up from all across the county and beyond for more than Independence Day this year.

Maybe independence from Hartstown having the wrong name for over a hundred years meant more to everyone than the mayor or anyone else expected. The horrifying and fascinating scandal of how Reginald Hart had made sure Mr. Boun and several others disappeared certainly made the rounds with lightning speed once it broke.

Beth's articles getting picked up from the local papers to run nationwide certainly helped.

Mark and Beth waited near a wooden staircase in the shadows beside the courthouse, both of them more twitchy and nervous than either Art or Melanie.

In fact, Art seemed completely in his element, dressed in a proper Southern pale blue cotton suit with a jaunty white bowtie. He hadn't been exactly shy about sharing the DNA results that confirmed he was indeed a descendant of Zachary Boun.

As far as Mark and the other two who knew the whole story were concerned, Art had more than earned the right to be proud of helping solve the mystery of Mr. Boun's disappearance all those years ago. And his eagerness to talk about the public side of it had encouraged a bunch more local folks to participate in DNA testing that got all the other bones identified and laid to rest with their families.

Melanie wore a bright green sundress that set off her red hair perfectly. And she had a new calm, a contentment as refreshing as the breeze carrying the scent of popcorn and hotdogs.

Mark thought she might be the only one whose life had changed as much as his and Beth's over the last year.

"You ready for this?" Beth said, probably sensing Mark's distinct *lack* of calm. Her light, billowy blouse and skirt matched her lovely blue eyes, and the effect had Mark a bit weak in the knees even after knowing her for several months.

Standing there with the three of them, he felt painfully underdressed in a forest green button-up shirt and black pants.

"I'm not sure why we're part of all this," he said. "Art and Melanie deserve the credit."

Beth rolled her eyes and reached for his hand. Clina's laugh echoed through his mind.

"I sure did hear what he said. He's the man for you all right, Beth, but he can be awful silly once in a while."

"Without you," Beth said, kissing Mark's cheek, "and me, and Clina Jane, and your Papaw, when would we have ever figured any of this out? Those bones and the stink and everything else would have stayed up there another hundred years. Now the whole county and half the country knows what really happened. And everyone who was trapped up there so long is resting easy alongside our miner, out in the cemetery where they should have been in the first place. Even their *teeth* are back where they belong."

"If you can't manage to take credit for anything else," Art said with a bemused smile, "at least think about getting Scatterland Creek cleaned up. Never would have managed that without you."

Mark shrugged and kicked at the grass, hoping he didn't look like the shy little boy he felt like right then. The lab technicians had wondered why he'd sent them a bag full of pure white moss, dead and rotted. He hadn't bothered to try to explain that it had been disturbingly alive and healthy when he gathered it a few hours before.

He definitely didn't argue when their tests of the water confirmed the arsenic and formaldehyde that shouldn't have been there at all, along with low oxygen and high methane and sulfur.

All of that had been enough to secure the funds to clean up the whole clear-cut site.

That cleanup included digging out Reginald Hart's huge, bizarre spell chamber, full of the bones of his murder victims and grave-robbed bodies of his supposed enemies. Creating a much larger opening and installing solar-powered fans cleared the methane gas and sulfur reek.

Melanie had successfully obliterated her Quad Great's lines and drawings with his own purifying white mud, but every single person who'd worked the site commented on how unsettled they were inside that cave.

Everyone also talked about how the cave and the creek and the hillsides covered with sapling hardwoods felt about a thousand times better now.

Permanent gas monitors hadn't caught a trace of elevated methane or sulfur in weeks.

And not a trace of the dead white remained along Scatterland Creek.

"I couldn't possibly thank all of you enough," Melanie said, a blush spreading across her delicate cheekbones. "Clearing out that cave got rid of more garbage inside my mind than you want to know about. Watching Bountyfield get its true name back today is just a bonus."

Art winked at Beth, then grinned at Mark and clapped him on the back.

"I hear from our friend Mr. Powell that you won't be going so long between visits anymore."

"You mean the visits I've been making every other weekend?" Mark said, laughing. He glanced at Beth, knowing she appreciated the time together as much as he did. Her flushed cheeks and shy smile proved it. "As it turns out, by the end of the month I won't be visiting Bountyfield at all anymore. I'll be living here."

Beth lifted her chin and looked Mark in the eye.

"That reminds me. Before we get called out to face the crowd, I wanted to ask you something."

Now Mark's heart sped up, and his own face heated. He'd been wanting to ask Beth a question, too. So much so that he'd spent a couple of hours talking to his Papaw about it the night before, snuggled close to Beth with a twitching Janie curled up against him.

The crowd noise, smells of grilling food, even Art and Melanie watching with knowing smiles faded away.

Leaving Mark focused on the person who mattered most in the world to him.

"Same here," he said. "You go first."

She ducked her head in the most enchanting way he could possibly imagine, then took his hand and looked back up at him.

"Assuming you don't have somewhere else already lined up," she said, "I was wondering if you might want to live with me for a while. You know, for Janie's sake. She misses you when you're gone."

Mark blinked, surprised at the simple, overwhelming joy of being asked. Even when neither of them had considered any other arrangement, being asked made the love between them official somehow.

But not as official as he wanted it to be.

"I think you're staring down your moment, water bug," his Papaw whispered.

"I miss Janie, too," Mark said. "And I can't think of anywhere else I'd want to live." His voice only shook a little, which was hard to believe with the way his heart thundered in his ears. "Don't married folks usually live together, though?"

Beth closed her eyes for a second before she grinned and nodded.

"That's what I hear. Are you asking me to marry you, Mark?"

Mark returned her grin and took a knee on the grass, exactly the way his Papaw told him he should.

"I sure am, even though I haven't had a chance to take

you ring shopping just yet. Nobody in this world or the next could suit me better."

"You're right about that." Beth pulled him to his feet and into a tight hug, squeezing the breath out of him with both arms. "You bet I'll let you take me ring shopping, but I don't care about that right now. As long as I've got you, I'm happy. Of *course* I'll marry you."

The cheers and laughter from Mark's Papaw, Clina, their rescued miner, Mr. Boun, and everyone else in the next world just about drowned out Art and Melanie's happy exclamations and hugs. As his surroundings filtered back in, Mark and everyone else realized the loud cheer from the front of the courthouse meant the mayor had started her speech.

And that she'd called them up to join her several seconds ago.

Mark wiped at his eyes, noticing the rest of them doing the same.

"Can't say I've got the best timing in the world," he said. "We're about to go public."

Art laughed, straightened his bowtie and smoothed his fuzz of hair.

"I'd say your timing is perfect, young man. One more new beginning to celebrate."

Mark brushed back his own unruly hair, grabbed Beth's hand, and walked with her into their future.

ABOUT KARI

The daughter, granddaughter, and great-granddaughter of coal miners, Kari Kilgore's wanderlust and imagination lead her all over the world on grand adventures. Her heart and family bring her home to her native Appalachian Mountains of Virginia. From that solid base, she and her husband Jason A. Adams bring those adventures to life in fiction.

Kari writes science fiction, fantasy, and horror, and she's happiest when she surprises herself. She lives at the end of a long dirt road in the middle of the woods with Jason, various house critters, and wildlife they're better off not knowing more about.

The Confidential Adventure Club

For Kari's exclusive free After The End stories and deleted scenes, discounts, early pre-sale releases, adorable pet photos, and a whole lot more not available anywhere else, visit The Confidential Adventure Club at www.smarturl.it/c-a-club.

Hope to see you there!

www.karikilgore.com
www.spiralpublishing.net

ALSO BY KARI KILGORE

I hope you enjoyed *Secrets in the Land* as much as I enjoyed writing it. Visiting with Mark, Beth, and Clina again was a real treat for me! If you haven't read *Songs in the Mountain*—the story of how Mark and Beth met, and how Beth met Clina—look for *Songs in the Mountain* and more of my fiction at www.karikilgore.com.

The Confidential Adventure Club

Want more fiction from Kari, including stories, discounts, and box sets not available anywhere else? Want to hear about locations, research, and other cool things that inspired this story and beyond? All that and adorable pet photos, too?

Join The Confidential Adventure Club and get a thank you gift of a free short story and a whole lot more at www.smarturl.it/c-a-club.

Hope to see you there!

The Storms of Future Past Series:

Dreaming the Storm

Joining the Storm

Into the Storm

Fighting the Storm

Sensing the Storm: A Storms of Future Past Prequel Story

Storms of Future Past Books One through Four Collection

The Voices through Time Series:

Songs in the Mountain

Secrets in the Land

Walking the Ghosts: A Voices through Time Novella

Dispatches from the Galaxy Stories:

Restricted Species

The Becalmed

The Garbage Belt

Terminalia Short Stories:

Terminalia

Little Five

Novels:

Until Death

The Dream Thief

Novellas:

Legacy of the Land

In the Pines

Collections:

Fantastic Women: A Dark Fantasy Novella Trio

Fantastic Shorts: Volume 1 - A Fantasy Short Story Collection

Near Future Forward (with Jason A. Adams)

Short Stories:

Intentions, The Seeds of Love, Wicked Bone, The Sound of Murder, Reflections, The Last Dragonkeeper, The Earworms

"Kari Kilgore is an author to watch—her lyrical voice a siren song; her insight, conjured voodoo."

—Richard Thomas, author of *Breaker* and *Tribulations*

www.ingramcontent.com/pod-product-compliance
Lightning Source LLC
Chambersburg PA
CBHW032038180726

48284CB00008B/2648